M Q

M

D1617424

GIRL FROM THE SEA

Carenza Pearce, eighteen, leaves the cottage where she was born to travel to Fistral Castle. She takes with her a letter of introduction from her late grandmother, but the owners of the castle turn her away angrily. Alone in the world and penniless, Carenza is talked into a marriage of convenience, but she soon discovers that much mystery surrounds the man she has married.

This is a tale of passion and intrigue in nineteenth-century Cornwall.

GIRL FROM THE SEA

Girl From The Sea

by
Ruth Abbey

Dales Large Print Books
Long Preston, North Yorkshire,
England.

British Library Cataloguing in Publication Data.

Abbey, Ruth
    Girl From The Sea.

    A catalogue record for this book is
    available from the British Library

    ISBN 1-85389-454-0 pbk

First published in Great Britain by Robert Hale Ltd., 1973

Copyright © 1973 by Ruth Abbey

Published in Large Print 1994 by arrangement with the copyright holder.

All rights reserved. No part of this publication may be reproduced, stored in a retrieval system, or transmitted in any form or by any means, electronic, mechanical, photocopying, recording or otherwise, without the prior permission of the Copyright owner.

Dales Large Print is an imprint of
Library Magna Books Ltd.
Printed and bound in Great Britain by
T.J. Press (Padstow) Ltd., Cornwall, PL28 8RW.

CHAPTER 1

It was a wild, fearful night. I got up from my chair beside the bed in which my grandmother was lying and peered anxiously out of the bedroom window. But it was as black as Hades itself out there in the night and I could see nothing but the cold, driving rain as it lashed and streamed down the small square panes. I could hear the pounding of the waves as they crashed with cruel fury on the rocks at the foot of the cliffs on which our cottage stood, and, far away, the mournful cry of a lone seagull. A sudden, swift despair engulfed me. Despondently I let the thin serge curtain fall back into place and turned the flickering oil lamp a little higher. I turned again to the frail figure in the bed; she was dying. My eyes brimming with tears, I looked down at her dear, beloved face, and I knew for certain that she would not see the morning.

Many times since I have asked myself how I could have been so sure, and to this day I do not know the answer. No one had told me she would die; no doctor had attended her. No one, in fact, had seen her but myself, for she had become ill only that afternoon. At the onset of her pain I had asked her to let me run up to the castle for help but she had replied indignantly: 'Have I brought you up these eighteen years, girl, and you know no better than to think I would have you go running for help at a mere twinge of pain; it is nothing I tell you; it will pass.'

But it had not passed. It had quickly worsened and in the end she had agreed to my going. And I had run through the wind and rain the mile along the cliff top and banged urgently on the castle door. Breathlessly I had stated my errand and waited anxiously while the butler had taken my message to Lord Tregonning, and thanked God when I was assured that *his lordship* would despatch someone at once to fetch a doctor.

But so far no doctor had arrived. I had raced back to the cottage to find my grandmother much worse. The pain itself, she said, was less severe, but I could see at once that she was weaker. And now, two hours later, the doctor had still not come, and she was sinking fast, barely conscious for most of the time.

I got up again from my chair and paced up and down the small room, pulling my shawl more closely around my shoulders. Even though I had lit a fire in the small black grate, the room was still cold and I went down the steep narrow stairs to fetch up more wood. I returned to find my grandmother struggling to raise herself up. I dropped the wood and ran across to her at once. She seemed to be trying to reach a small wooden box stood on the table beside her bed. Her thin work-worn hands groped over the bedclothes and she kept muttering. 'The chest, Carenza, the chest.'

I picked it up and gave it to her but she was too weak to hold it, 'Open it,' she whispered urgently. 'Open it.'

I tried at once to do her bidding but the chest was locked. She pointed to a drawer in her dressing-table and there I found a small brass key. It turned smoothly in the lock and as it did a strange feeling of apprehension surged through me. Before I raised the lid I looked at Grandmother. She had sunk among the pillows, her eyes closed, and she seemed to have lapsed into unconsciousness again. My hands trembling nervously I slowly opened the chest. Inside were two letters. One was addressed to me and bore simply the word *Carenza,* the other was addressed to someone I had never heard of in my life. Unable almost to believe my eyes I said the words aloud: *'To Sir Rupert Harford—or whoever it may concern, Fistral Castle, North Cornwall.'*

The sound of my voice must have roused Grandmother for she opened her eyes, and pointing a gnarled finger at the letter addressed to me, mouthed the word 'Read.' As I opened the envelope and drew out the folded piece of paper within, I was surprised to see that the letter was not old; it was dated only two weeks previously and had been written by my grandmother herself.

My heart pounded with a disturbing, inexplicable fear, I began to read; my hands shook so much that I could not hold the paper still, and I had to lay the letter down on the table beside the bed before I could see the writing properly. This is what I read:

My dear Carenza,

Today something has happened which has made me see that soon you must be told the truth; several times during these last months, since your eighteenth birthday in fact, I have been on the verge of telling you as much as I knew, and now, what I have seen this day has finally decided me. You are not, as you have always supposed yourself to be, my grand-daughter; you are not even a relative. How you came to be born in this cottage is a strange and puzzling story; the only person who could have explained the mystery was your mother and she alas, God rest her soul, died in giving birth to you.

This is what happened: there had been a wicked storm, a storm which raged for two whole days and nights, and when at last it died away, my daughter and her husband who, as you know, shared this cottage, went down the cliffs searching for driftwood. They saw your mother lying among the rocks at the mouth of one of the caves. At first they thought she was dead: her small elfin face was white as marble, and her eyes were closed. When they reached her they saw that she was heavy with child and from the faint moaning noise coming through her drained lips, that she was alive.

How she came to be lying there we shall never know; there had been ships wrecked further up the coast during the storm and she may have been a survivor, washed into our cove by the tide; certainly her clothing clung wet and sodden about her. And yet, her long black hair, which my daughter described as being *'spread out like a soft dark cloud behind her head'*, was dry to the touch. It may be that she walked to the cove and was overcome by exhaustion, and this is what I myself believe, for her boots were worn and thin as though she had walked in them for many miles.

My son-in-law carried her up to the cottage and when I saw them coming I thought it was a child he bore in his arms, for she was no taller than a child and as fragile and slight of frame. Even carrying a child within her womb, she was as a feather in my son-in-law's strong arms. As soon as they laid her down on the bed I could see that her time would soon be upon her; she was moaning quietly and once or twice uttered strange, foreign-sounding words. It was clear to me she had a fever of some kind.

My daughter and I made her as comfortable as we could and took turns in sitting beside her. There was no one on whom we could call for help for his lordship was in foreign parts and the castle closed up for the winter. And so we did what we could for the poor luckless child, for that is all she seemed, and when, the next day, you were born, she died. There seemed to be no strength left in her, no fight, it was almost as though she had given up the struggle to go on living.

We tried to find out about her and asked her where she came from and where she was bound, but so great was her fever she seemed either not to hear or not to understand. Once or twice during her labour she muttered to herself but again some of the words were foreign to us and even those of our own tongue did not make any sense to us. One word alone we were able to understand and that was a name, Rupert. She whispered it as she died.

We buried her in the copse behind the cottage, knowing only one thing about her, her name; for round her neck and close to her heart, hung a locket, a little heart-shaped silver trinket with the name—a foreign-sounding name and one not known in these parts, Elaine Van Luther inscribed upon it...

The writing was blotched here as though something wet had touched the page. Tears, I told myself, as my own spilled over and added to the blotches. Swallowing hard I continued to read—

Inside the locket was a picture of a young gentleman. We examined it closely to see if any name were written there, but there was no writing upon it whatsoever.

As for you my child, we named you Carenza for had my daughter been able to bear the child she longed for, that is how she would have named a daughter. We brought you up as our own. My daughter and her husband loved you as their own flesh and blood, as I do. When the sea took them from me in the great storm twelve years ago, you were the only thing left for me to live for...but I have to tell you the truth now...

Your poor dear mother, alas, wore no wedding ring upon her finger, but nevertheless, I believed that she was a good woman and that you are a lady, and highly born. Before I married, I was governess to a noble family in Devon and I am conversant with the mien and manners of well bred people. From your earliest years it has been apparent to me that you are different from folk like us...there is a quality and an air of breeding about you which I could not fail to recognise.

And now today when I took the linen to the castle, I saw the picture...the maid who takes the sheets to the great cupboards upstairs is sick and so I was sent along the long landings and there it was, a picture staring down at me, the very image of the young gentleman in the locket... Fearful lest anyone should see me I peered closely and read the name beneath that handsome face...it was Sir Rupert Harford. Perhaps you noticed when I came home tonight that I am all upset and excited...perhaps you wondered at my silence, my air of preoccupation...but the truth is that I have been torn by indecision...should I tell his lordship about the locket and the picture...should I tell you about them...what is my duty to you? But if I do, will they take you away from me...I think it more than probable...that they would...

Here it seemed to me there was a pause in the letter, as if my grandmother had stopped writing for a while; there was, in fact, a gap in the lines of neat sloping script and as I looked at the letter more closely I saw that a second date had been inserted. I looked back at the first date and saw that the second one was but a day later. The letter continued:

I have worried all night about what I should do and have at last made up my mind. The letter with this one, as you will see, is addressed to Sir Rupert Harford; inside it is the locket found on your mother, and all the information I have just imparted to you. The man, Sir Rupert, may know of your mother, who her people were and where she came from; he may even be a relative and I pray that it is so; in any event he has a kind face and will, I pray, help you.

Let me warn you here my little Carenza not to harbour any false hope that he may be your father as such a notion will only bring you disappointment: as I have already told you, your mother wore no wedding ring.

Take this letter to Sir Rupert yourself;

his lordship will tell you about boarding the coach, and the money for the journey you will find in my leather purse. I pray it will be sufficient. It is all that I have. I am an old woman now and it cannot be long before the Angel of Death calls me and so I have written all this down now in order that when the time comes for me to go, all will be ready for you; for I have faced the fact that I cannot bear to part with you, and until I die the secret will remain mine alone.

God forgive me, if, in my desire to keep you by my side, I have wronged you. When you read this letter my dearest child, I shall be dead.

Through my tears I looked at my grandmother; she was dead. The letter fluttered from my hand and fell to the floor; mechanically I picked it up, folded it and put it back with the other one in the chest. I leaned over and kissed my grandmother for the last time; an overwhelming ache consumed me and for hours it seemed I was incapable of either movement or thought.

It was only when the grey light of dawn came creeping up over the sea that I became conscious that my limbs were stiff with cold and that I had sat beside the bed all through the night. Strangely, I felt no fear in the presence of death, but the sorrow of parting from the one who had been my world for the past twelve years was like a physical pain. I realised that I must pull myself together. I tidied the bed and cleaned out the grate. Then I went downstairs and washed at the pump in the scullery, and combed my long black hair. Doing things with my hands seemed to bring some small measure of solace to my grief-stricken heart and so I busied myself with all manner of unnecessary tasks until it was light enough for me to go to the castle.

Lord Tregonning was kind and good; he arranged for my grandmother's burial and gave me a room in the servants' quarters until after the funeral; he arranged too for the sale of the few sticks of furniture in the cottage for me.

'What will you do, child?' he asked me kindly, after handing me the pittance it had fetched. 'There is little here, and I do not imagine your grandmother had much else to leave you. Have you anywhere to go? There is work for you at the castle if you wish for it.'

'Thank you, my lord,' I replied most gratefully. 'It is kind of you to offer me a position in your household, but I have somewhere to go...' I hesitated, unwilling for some reason to tell him the truth about myself... 'My grandmother requested me to go to the North Cornwall coast...and there is enough money for me to make the journey.'

'You have relatives on the northern coast?'

I hesitated once more before replying: 'Yes, my lord,' I had not forgotten my grandmother's warning not to harbour false hopes regarding my relationship with Sir Rupert, but ever since I had read her letter, a secret hope had begun to burn within me.

Lord Tregonning was speaking again; he was, I thought, relieved at my answer. 'Then that is the place for you,' he beamed, 'with your own people.' He turned to leave me.

'Just one more thing, if you please, my lord,' I cried after him. 'I would be greatly obliged if you would tell me where and at what hour I can board a coach for my journey.'

'Twelve noon tomorrow,' he told me

19

promptly, 'at the Falcon Inn in the town.'

I curtsied and took my leave of him.

Early next morning I set out to walk the seven or so miles into the town. As I journeyed I pondered upon my situation, wondering what the future held in store for me. My heart was still heavy with sorrow and loneliness, and yet deep down, a faint stirring of hope moved within me...parts of my grandmother's letter kept dancing before my eyes, the letter that had turned all my ideas about myself upside down...could it be true, I wondered with a feeling that was a mixture of hopeful expectancy and awe, that I, poverty stricken though I might be, was a lady... a lady of noble birth...

About half way upon my journey I heard the sound of a horse's hooves behind me, and turning saw a big black horse thundering towards me. The rider, hatless, his cloak billowing out in the wind behind him, was bent low over the horse's head. A little afraid, for I had heard many stories of smugglers and highwaymen and their nefarious deeds, I started to run, glancing behind me fearfully as I did so. It was a rough road with many loose stones, and in my agitation I was not careful of my steps.

Without warning I stumbled over a jagged piece of rock and fell flat on my face in the middle of the road and right in the path of the flying hooves behind me.

With a curse the rider pulled his horse to a standstill within inches of where I lay.

'What the devil do you think you're doing, young woman?' he demanded in an angry, impatient voice. 'Throwing yourself in front of my mare in such a fashion.'

Dazed from the savage blow my head had suffered, I looked up to see a tall, dark-haired man, blue eyes blazing with annoyance, glaring down at me. With as much dignity as I could muster, I struggled to my feet and replied evenly: 'I did *not* throw myself in front of your horse; I fell over a loose stone, as surely you must have realised, I put my hand to my forehead where I could feel the blood trickling and turned my back on him. I desperately wanted to get away from him but as I took a step forward I swayed and almost fell down again. At once the stranger was beside me, steadying me with a vice-like grip on my arm.

'You are hurt,' he announced, his tone still curt, 'your head bleeds, you had better rest for a while.'

'I would prefer to continue on my journey,' I replied with a terseness to equal his own. 'If you will kindly leave go of my arm I will do so. I must be in the town by noon.'

'Don't be such a damned little idiot,' he retorted furiously. 'Do as you are told and rest; I am not accustomed to having my orders disobeyed.'

Still a little afraid I made no demur as he led me to a large boulder at the side of the road. Once there, he took from his cloak a handkerchief and dabbed my wound. I stole a glance at him from beneath my lowered eyelids; I was still uncertain what manner of person he might be: true, his voice was cultured and his speech that of a gentleman, but there was something wild and reckless about him, a devil-may-care glint to the sea-blue eyes, that troubled me not a little. Instinctively my hand closed tightly on the leather purse in the pocket of my cloak. I wished he would go away.

As soon as I felt a little steadier, I thanked him for his attentions and added that I did not wish to delay him and that I was perfectly all right again.

'Well, you do not look alright,' he told me, glaring down at me. 'You look white and shaken and much too frail to walk any further. You are a confounded nuisance and have caused me to waste time I can ill afford to lose; but damn you, I cannot leave you to journey alone in such a state; there is but one remedy.'

'And what is that, sir?' I asked, alarmed suddenly by something in his tone and in his eyes.

'This,' he announced, and, before I could possibly divine his intention, he lifted me bodily into the saddle and swung himself up behind me.

CHAPTER 2

The memory of that journey will live with me for always. The speed and suddenness with which the stranger acted momentarily took my breath away, but as soon as I could speak I cried angrily: 'Put me down at once; how dare you behave in so high-handed a manner?'

'Dare?' he echoed, 'Dare? There is nothing in the world I dare not do. As for putting you down, certainly not—and you may just as well stop struggling. Why, I could pinion you fast with one arm, little slip of a thing that you are.' And suiting the action to his words he held me firmly around the waist with one arm and flicking the reins with his free hand, set his horse to a gallop. I had never been so angry or so frightened in my whole life, but I realised that it was pointless to argue with him further; such a course would only be futile. Holding myself stiffly and away from him as much as I possibly could, I lapsed into silence.

Reluctantly I was forced to admire his horsemanship, for he had absolute control of the mare which in turn responded to the slightest touch of knees and rein. As the road we were following ran perilously close to the cliff edge in many places, I was relieved that this was so, for at the reckless speed we were going, the slightest misjudgement could have meant disaster. Once he bent his head close to my ear and shouted above the wind to ask if I was afraid. Without turning I shook my head, and heard him laugh with disbelief.

'Your heart belies you little one,' he cried mockingly. 'You forget, I can feel it fluttering like a bird against me.' And he laughed again.

Blushing furiously I made no answer, and prayed for the journey to end quickly. I kept hoping that we might encounter someone on the road so that I could call for help but we met no one. Gradually, however, my fears began to subside a little and the wild beating of my heart calm down, for it seemed clear that this man had no evil intent towards me, at least for the time being, and soon we must reach the town where there would be people abroad.

Sure enough as we reached the next bend in the road I could see, looking down, the huddle of houses and cottages at the foot of the cliffs. As we descended, the stranger seemed to hold me more tightly against him, a circumstance which began to arouse my apprehension again, until I realised the steepness of the gradient we were going down. Obviously he was merely protecting me against accident. Such a thought served to cool my anger against him just a little and by the time we entered the town I was completely calm.

'Here we are!' the stranger announced. 'And with but ten minutes to spare.'

He reined in his horse and without dismounting lifted me unceremoniously to the ground. 'Take care of that head,' he shouted down to me. 'And in future look where you're going; apart from the fact that you have been a confounded nuisance to me, you might well have hurt yourself badly.' And with this he dug his heels into the flanks of the horse and galloped off out of my sight.

My head was beginning to throb, partly I believed from vexation at the man's unreasonable words. But I had no time to do anything about it for it was essential that I should set about finding the coaching inn. Luckily I had been put down not far from it and was directed there by an old woman sitting in the doorway of her cottage.

''Tis round the corner,' she replied in answer to my question, eyeing me curiously at the same time.

'Thank you.' I smiled and set off the way she pointed.

'You'm wisht.' She was staring at the scratch on my forehead.

'No,' I told her. 'It is nothing and doesn't bother me.'

She shook her head as if in disbelief.

'Wisht,' she said again, 'And you'm thin as a rake.'

I hurried away from her prying eyes and soon reached the Falcon Inn. I have never seen such a place in all my life; everywhere was stir and bustle: doors were opening and shutting, bells ringing, and people rushing hither and thither all the time. Everybody, it seemed, was in a hurry. Some like the old woman, eyed me curiously and I became uncomfortably aware that I must appear somewhat dishevelled.

There was a boy cleaning boots out in the yard and a woman carrying an armful of clean linen, approaching the door. The sight of her reminded me of my grandmother and I had a hard struggle not to give way to a fit of weeping.

Fortunately the coach arrived at that time, wheeling under the gateway with a clangour that made the roof ring. There were several people waiting to board it. Many of them turned out to be outside passengers and as I watched them climbing up into their places I felt pity for them, for it was an intensely cold day; they would surely need their coats and shawls and mufflers they were wrapped in.

Glad that I had sufficient money for an

inside seat, I climbed into the coach. There was but one other occupant and this was a lady of, I guessed, about twenty-five or six years. She was magnificently attired in a travelling habit of brown velvet and fur and beautiful to look at. Her fair hair was fashionably dressed in a way similar to that of her ladyship at the castle and her skin was creamy-white and flawless. She turned her big green eyes upon me as I sat down, but she gave me no welcoming smile and the friendly overture I had been about to make died in my throat. For perhaps half a mile she stared at me rudely, taking in, I expect, every detail of my humble attire and my appearance and then she yawned and looked out of the window in a bored fashion. It was clear that she had no intention of conversing with me, and in fact she did not utter a single word. It did not worry me at all, although I thought her very haughty looking, because I had many things on my mind that I wished to think about.

First and foremost of these was my grandmother's letter. I did not need to look at it again, although it was readily to hand in my valise, for the words were engraved on my heart. I tried, as I had tried so many times since I had first found out the truth about myself, to picture my mother. From the letter I had gleaned really so little about her. I knew that she was small and slight and had had long black hair, but that was all. I did not even know the colour of her eyes. Were they, I wondered, brown like mine, or were they perhaps green like the haughty woman's opposite me, or blue like the stranger's, blue as a Cornish sea on a sunny day...thinking on such lines brought his face vividly before me for a moment and I was a little startled at how clearly it had become imprinted on my mind.

My anger against him had completely evaporated by this time for I had come to realise that but for his setting me upon his horse with him, I should have missed the coach. Strange man, I mused: arrogant, rude, ill-tempered and yet oddly gentle. But what of it? What matter what manner of man he was. It was almost certain I would never encounter him again in the whole of my life.

But in making such an assumption I could not have been more mistaken, as I was very soon to find out.

Some little way before we reached the second inn along the route, I became aware of a change in my companion. Her boredom seemed to vanish and I noticed that she took from her muff a small mirror, and studied her reflection carefully for some minutes. Apparently satisfied with what the mirror had shown, she started to look about through the carriage windows with interest, and a slight smile curved her full red lips. I concluded that she was nearing her destination and looking forward, perhaps, to being back home with her husband or her parents again.

But when the coach pulled up at the inn, to my surprise, she made no move to leave it. The smile on her face widened and then turned to a look of vexed incredulity when she saw that there was no one waiting to board the coach; as a couple of the outside passengers climbed down from their places, she leaned from the window, looking this way and that way about the inn yard. A frown creased her white forehead and she drummed impatiently on the seat beside her with her exquisitely gloved fingers. It seemed clear that she had been expecting someone to join her at this stage of her journey.

'Wait!' she commanded the coachman imperiously. 'Climb down again. There is a passenger for this coach and you *must* wait. Something must have delayed him.'

The coachman began to argue volubly but I thought it more than likely that she failed to understand the dialect which rolled from his tongue.

'Stop your ranting, man,' she ordered. 'If you leave this passenger behind, believe me you will be sorry; he is a most important personage.'

The man, still grumbling in his broad Cornish, got down from his seat. As he did so, a man on horseback rode hurriedly into the inn yard, handed over his horse to a stable lad, and strode towards the coach. At first I did not recognise him for the clothes he was wearing were much more splendid than those he had worn when I had last seen him, but as he opened the door of the coach and climbed inside, I saw, with a start of amazement, that it was the stranger. He seemed equally surprised to see me.

'Well,' he cried, 'if it isn't the waif of the cliff road again. What trouble will you cause on this part of my journey, I wonder?'

I lowered my gaze away from the mocking blue eyes and murmured that

I had no intention of being a trouble to anyone. Her expression a mixture of amazement and annoyance, the haughty woman looked from one to the other of us.

'Am I to understand, Nicholas, that you actually know this person?' she demanded of the stranger. A smile played round his mouth as he replied. 'You are indeed, my dear Penelope; not only do I know this young lady, I have also had the pleasure of her company when riding.'

I blushed furiously at his words and looked down at my feet in embarrassment, but not before I had seen the look of disbelieving anger which flashed across his companion's face.

'Indeed,' she commented icily. 'But then of course, Nicholas, you definitely are the strangest man, with, if I may say so, rather...' She hesitated, and then finished, 'rather unusual tastes in many ways.' Her face was wreathed in a smile and her green eyes held a provocative glint as she looked at the stranger. The insult behind her words, though veiled, was pointed and the barb went home; my colour deepened still further but I found myself completely incapable of replying in the same manner.

Nicholas, it seemed, suffered from no such inhibitions.

'Pray tell me,' he drawled, 'what is strange about enjoying the company of a pretty woman?'

'Oh Nicholas, you really are incorrigible,' came the reply. 'You can never be serious about anything, I'm afraid.'

'I have never been more serious in my life,' he told her blandly, the most innocent-looking expression covering his face. Penelope seemed on the point of arguing further and then obviously thinking better of it, murmured:

'You're impossible,' smiling at him archly again.

Throughout their banter I had felt embarrassed and uncomfortable; slightly angry too, for Lady Penelope had behaved almost as if I were not present, or at best were someone of absolutely no consequence, whose feelings need not be considered in the least. The only comfort I found was in the fact that the stranger had undoubtedly got the better of her in the argument and that she had not in the least enjoyed the exchange between them. For some reason I felt sure that the stranger had been deliberately trying to provoke her and had very nearly succeeded; in fact that he *had* succeeded but that she was too clever a person to reveal the fact.

I fell to speculating about the relationship between them and my instinct told me at once that the lady was extremely attracted to her companion, but as regards his feelings towards her I could not be at all so sure...he did not seem to behave like a man in love...or at least how I imagined a man in love would behave...the man who had loved my mother for instance, the man who was my father...he would have looked and spoken in a very different way... The man who would one day love me...

'What a dreamer you are! No wonder you fell over a rock.' The words brought me back to reality with a start. 'It is a good thing that you are not in charge of the coach, Miss Whatever your name is.'

I looked across to find the bold blue eyes upon me once more. 'My name is Carenza Pearce,' I supplied. I had decided to keep to my grandmother's surname, the one by which I had always been known, at least for the time being and until I could establish my true identity if such a thing were possible.

'Pearce,' he echoed. 'A good old Cornish name like my own.' He gave a mockery of a bow: 'I am Tangye—Nicholas Tangye and this, my companion here, is Lady Penelope Tresidder—a fairly near neighbour of mine.'

As courtesy demanded, I inclined my head towards both of them but Lady Penelope ignored my overture completely. She changed the subject and soon they were deep in discussion of people and places of whom and of which I had never heard, a conversation in which I could not possibly join.

I gave all my attention to the passing scenery. In the distance I could see a large mule train plodding its way over a moorland track, each animal laden with two sacks which hung on either side of a pack-saddle. Their drivers, I noticed, were walking behind, and the mules seemed to be picking their own way, more or less as they chose. I supposed they would be on their way from some mine or other to one of the ports. A man on horseback, a woman (his wife presumably) and a child perched up behind him on a pillion, came riding towards us, and I could hear some of the outside passengers calling a greeting to the travellers as we passed by them.

Suddenly, something my companions were saying riveted my attention. 'So you made the coach wait for me?' Nicholas Tangye was saying. 'What puzzles me not a little, Penelope, is how the devil you knew I was going to travel by it.'

Lady Penelope's gaze did not meet his as she replied: 'Oh, quite by chance really, Nicholas. I had a letter from Marion Harford whilst I was in Falmouth. She mentioned that you were staying with the Pendarves and that you were returning to Trenance House today—'

'And how the devil did *she* know, may I ask?' His voice was sardonic.

'Oh, your housekeeper apparently told the Fistral Castle housekeeper.'

'Ah. Women. I might have known. Forever prattling about affairs that do not concern them.'

'I agree absolutely,' Lady Penelope said promptly. 'Women of the lower classes are incorrigible gossips and busybodies.' She looked across in my direction with a meaning that was all too obvious.

'*All* women, damn them,' muttered her companion. 'I have yet to meet one who

36

could control her tongue.'

Lady Penelope laughed with feigned good humour, shaking her head at him playfully.

Lady Penelope's mention of the name Marion Harford had interested me greatly. Could she be, I wondered, the wife of the Sir Rupert to whom my grandmother's letter was addressed, or his daughter perhaps? It seemed probable.

Had Lady Penelope been a more agreeable person I might have ventured to ask her about the Harfords and about Fistral Castle, but as it was I did not dare, having a good notion as to the kind of rebuff I might suffer. The bit about the housekeepers had interested me, too. It would appear then that Mr Nicholas Tangye's residence was not so very far from Fistral Castle. Should it turn out that I was to make my future home at the castle, I might meet him again some time. Strange though the man undoubtedly was, the idea was not disagreeable...

We were approaching an inn. When the coach halted on the cobblestones, the coachman climbed down, and opening the door, informed me kindly that this was where I must alight for Fistral Castle.

'Fistral Castle?' The amazement in Lady Penelope's voice was almost comical. '*You* are going to Fistral Castle?' she stopped then laughed maliciously before continuing: 'But of course, how stupid of me; Marion said they were taking on extra servants.'

Somewhere deep inside me something flared. I got up from my seat, and indignation burning in my voice I told her: 'It may interest you to know that I do *not* journey to Fistral Castle seeking employment. I visit there for private and personal reasons.' I turned towards Nicholas Tangye. 'As for you, sir,' I said hotly, 'if you are an honest man, I think you will admit that at last you have encountered a woman who *can* control her tongue. Under the circumstances I consider I have controlled mine admirably.'

Red in the face and not a little amazed at my own temerity, I picked up my valise and left them. Never to my dying day shall I forget the look on Lady Penelope's face. As I walked towards the inn, head held high, I heard Nicholas Tangye's laughter ringing through the coach. The sound of it pleased me.

CHAPTER 3

The coach went on its way again and I went into the inn. There were two matters that I needed to enquire about: one was to ask whether my trunk (a small one) containing all my possessions could stay at the inn until such time as I could arrange to have it fetched to Fistral Castle, and the other one was to ask the way to Fistral Castle.

'Fistral Castle?' the landlord repeated. ' 'Tis by the sea some two or three miles from 'ere; a purty step et is, but ee'll not miss et; stands high on the cliffs et do.'

I thanked him and asked about my trunk. He looked at me curiously, as if, I thought, he would have liked to find out more about me and ask a few questions about my visit to the castle. However, he evidently decided against such a course and merely nodded, indicating to the manservant who had lifted it down from the coach for me, where to store it.

As I walked across the inn yard to

set off on my journey, noise and chatter coming from a long, low building to the right attracted my attention. Curious, I peeped inside and discovered that it was a kayle alley. I looked more closely for I had often heard my grandmother speak of this game which was a favourite pastime of the miners, but I had never seen it in progress before; there was a plank floor and seats on either side of the playing space; the pins were about twelve inches high and were furnished with iron collars which made a tremendous clatter when they were knocked down. There seemed to be a lot of drinking going on at the same time as the play and I remembered my grandmother's talk of how the game was usually played for a wager such as a barrel of beer. A staunch Methodist, Grandmother had disapproved of this sort of behaviour, declaring that most times the men got so drunk they became like animals. Looking at those in the alley before me, I could see well what she meant. I turned away and began to walk briskly in the direction of Fistral Castle. As the afternoon wore on the cold became more severe and there was an added damp feeling in the air which chilled me. I walked as quickly as the rutted, muddy road would allow, swinging my arms from time to time in an effort to warm myself up a little.

After I had been going for perhaps an hour, I saw the castle; as the landlord had prophesied it was impossible to miss it. A great mass of grey sticking up on the skyline; the sight of it filled me with awe and for the first time since I had embarked on my journey, I began to be fearful of the outcome. What was I about, presenting myself to strangers—strangers who lived in style such as this? What would they say to me? How would they receive me? The only right that I had to approach them at all was the letter from my grandmother, and the locket. But supposing the picture in the locket was *not* that of Sir Rupert Harford? What then?

I shivered at the thought. Grandmother had been an old woman, her eyesight had been failing; she had truly believed that the picture and the likeness in the locket were of the same man but she could have been mistaken. My spirits sank as I faced the very real possibility that this might indeed be so. I tried to cheer myself up with the thought that Grandmother had said that Sir Rupert had a kind face. 'Dear God,' I prayed as I drew nearer and nearer to the castle, 'please let him deal kindly with me.'

I could hear the sea now and see the waves pounding the rocks far below the castle. It stood on a sort of headland, the sea surrounding the grounds on three sides, and it was even larger and more extensive than I had thought. Trembling with nervousness I made my way to one of the great doors. I did not know which one of them I ought to go to, so I made for the nearest one, hoping desperately that I had not made some great error. At the last minute I almost lost my courage and turned and fled from the place, but willing myself to behave sensibly and with dignity, I raised my hand to the knocker. My heart in my mouth, I waited for the great door to open.

After less than a minute it did so, and a manservant enquired my business. He eyed me curiously but treated me with politeness. I took a deep breath:

'I wish to see Sir Rupert Harford,' I announced in as firm and calm a tone as I could muster. 'I have a letter of introduction from,' I hesitated, then finished, 'from a friend.'

A look of surprise flashed across the man's face at my words. 'Sir Rupert is dead, missie,' he told me, 'and has been these last fifteen years.'

'Dead?' I echoed stupidly. 'Dead?' Of all the differing possibilities I had imagined, this one, really the most likely of all, had never once occurred to me. 'Dead,' I repeated flatly once more and turned away from the door, my shoulders drooped in disappointment.

'Wait, young missie.' It was the servant calling after me. 'I will go and ask if young Sir William or the mistress will see you. Please to step inside,' he added kindly. 'You are cold and tired.'

Gratefully I followed him into the great hall. He pointed to a wooden chair. 'Sit 'ee down,' he whispered. 'Sit 'ee down.'

I smiled my thanks and sank gratefully onto the chair; I was indeed both cold and tired and feeling faint from want of food, for I had not eaten all day. The coach journey had considerably lessened the money in my leather purse and I had not dared to spend any on food, lest I should need what was left for a night's lodging.

It was gloomy in the great hall and had I not been so cold I think I might have fallen asleep where I was. I did in fact feel my eyelids drooping for a moment, but was suddenly jerked wide awake by a peculiar feeling that someone was watching me. I sat up straight in my chair and looked about me but I could see no one; then a sound, no more than a rustle, caught my ears. It came, I thought, from the direction of the minstrels' gallery at the far end of the hall and as I glanced upwards I caught sight of someone peering through the carved woodwork.

In the waning light of late afternoon the hall was dark, full of shadows, and though I strained my eyes to the uttermost, I could not at first determine exactly who or what it was that watched me. But as my eyes became accustomed to the gloom I was able to see that it was a woman who crouched there, up in the gallery. Through the balustrades I caught a glimpse of grey hair, long and dishevelled, a white face...I moved nearer and looked up. Even in the gloom, the wildness in the eyes looking down into mine was unmistakable. I shivered and took a step backwards. The woman put a finger to her lips and vanished behind a pillar.

I walked back to my chair instinctively aware that I was still being watched by the now unseen watcher...it was a feeling which did not increase my confidence...I wondered who the strange-looking woman could be and what sort of household it was whose thick grey walls I had entered...

The appearance of the young master put an end to my speculations. I disliked him on sight. He eyed me up and down disdainfully as I jumped to my feet. 'Yes?' he asked coldly.

Wordlessly, I took the letter from my valise and handed it to him. My hands shook so much I could hardly close the fastener. His cold grey eyes appraising me, he took the large white envelope I held out to him. As he opened it I studied him covertly. He was a small man, not much taller than myself and inclined to stoutness. His face was round, the skin white and pasty-looking and his hands were fat with short, thick fingers; sparse, gingerish hair and a weak, receding chin, did nothing to enhance his appearance.

I judged him to be about forty or thereabouts. He was unfolding the square piece of paper, peering closely at it as though he were short-sighted. I watched him anxiously. Not a flicker of expression crossed his face as he read what my grandmother had written.

'You know the contents of this letter?' he asked curtly, at length.

'No, sir, not exactly,' I replied truthfully. 'My grandmother told me the gist of what she had written to you, but I have not read the letter—nor have I seen the locket.'

Up to this point he had, as far as I could tell, given the locket only a cursory glance, holding it in his hand unopened. He turned now to the manservant. 'Leave us,' he commanded.

The man withdrew, casting a sympathetic look in my direction as he did so; silently I blessed him. In the face of the coldness I was receiving from the master of the castle, it was a kindly gesture sorely needed and much appreciated. The little silver locket clicked open in Sir William's podgy hand; he held it up towards the light which filtered in from the windows high in the rough stone walls. Again I watched him closely, anxiously, for any sign that he recognised the face in the locket, but he gave none. My heart sank to the depths.

Truly my grandmother had been mistaken. I waited for him to say something. I thought he was on the point of speaking when suddenly there was an interruption. A high-pitched voice, a woman's voice, called from somewhere at the other end of the great hall.

'William,' she shrieked, 'I have been looking all over the castle for you—' she stopped abruptly as approaching Sir William she saw me. Turning towards him her eyes went to the opened letter in his hand, to the locket. 'What is it?' she asked sharply. 'What does this person want?' casting a cursory glance in my direction. 'And why wasn't I informed at once?'

'It is nothing for you to trouble about,' Sir William replied in a curt tone. 'I did not call you because there was no point in doing so.' He made as if to put the letter in a pocket of his richly brocaded coat, but she snatched it away from him.

'Let me see,' she whined. She opened the letter out again and her eyes went quickly over the small, neat lines of writing. Her face, as she read, took on, I thought, a startled, apprehensive look. Sir William seemed nervous and annoyed.

'I told you it was nothing for you to

bother your head about, Marion,' he said impatiently. 'I will deal with the matter.'

His words were ignored. 'The locket,' she asked. 'Give it to me, William. I wish to see it.'

'There is no point,' hedged her husband. 'It has all been a mistake.' He was looking into his wife's face now in a careful, meaningful way and I received the distinct impression that he was desperately trying to convey something to her without putting it into words; it was almost as though he were trying to warn her of something... She took no notice, seemingly, and held out her heavily ringed hand for the locket.

'Come over here towards the light,' Sir William moved away from the two of us as he spoke. 'You will see the trinket much more clearly over here.'

She gave him a puzzled glance from her dull grey eyes but followed him to where he stood some few yards away. It was now not so easy for me to observe her reaction but, when she finally opened the locket, although I could not discern exactly the expression in her eyes, there was no mistaking the gasp of amazement, quickly smothered, which escaped her. I waited, almost with bated breath for what she had to say, for I was fairly certain that she recognised the picture inside that locket. She snapped it shut with a decisive movement and handing it back to her husband said hurriedly, 'You are absolutely right, William. There has been a mistake. I have never seen this—this—person. I wish I had done as you requested and not wasted my time on such a matter.' She swept away then, her brown silk skirt rustling, pausing only to look me full in the face as she passed by me. There was hate in her eyes and fear... Alarmed and greatly puzzled, I stared back at her. Her plain square face was as white as death.

When she had gone, Sir William turned on me furiously. 'I could have you thrown into prison for this outrage,' he shouted. 'Trumping up some ridiculous story that you may be our relative.' He laughed harshly and without mirth. 'You,' he went on scathingly. *You!* Why, you're nothing but a servant girl. As for this cheap trinket here, I expect your grandmother either stole or found it somewhere. I can see it all. She judged the picture to be that of a gentleman and as she had doubtless heard of our family being one of the richest and most important in the country, decided to

It was then I heard the laughter. It rang out from the castle, a long maniacal peal, wild and terrifying. I set off down the long drive as fast as my legs would carry me, away from that horrible, inhuman sound.

When I reached the road again I stopped to get my breath and to think about what I could do. It was fast becoming dark and I knew I must make up my mind quickly. There seemed but one course open to me and that was to make my way back to the inn. I knew that I had enough money left for a night's lodging and was thankful that I had not spent it on food. The thought of the long wearying journey ahead of me almost overwhelmed me, for I was chilled to the bone and most desperately tired. With a heavy heart I set off. I was thankful to be walking away from the sea, from the sound of the waves which, driven by the howling gale lashed the rocks with unabated fury.

The wind tore at my face, wrenching the breath from my throat, as head down, I battled along the lonely road, willing myself to keep moving. Any thoughts and speculations about my future that I might have reflected upon, receded to the back of my mind in my struggle against the elements. My one concern was to reach the inn. Shelter and food, those were my immediate and urgent needs; later I would consider my future. I think it was because of this that I gave no thought to the possible dangers of my journey; danger from robbers or highwaymen that I might encounter. But even if these fears had presented themselves to me, I doubt if I should have heeded them; that I should reach the inn as soon as I possibly could, outweighed all other considerations. But as the distance between me and the comparative safety of the castle precincts became wider and wider, little stabs of unease began to unnerve me.

The rough track was now crossing through lonely, bleak countryside with little or no cover where one could hide from an assailant. Instinctively I quickened my pace, those first stirrings of fear lending renewed strength to my weary limbs. But suddenly I heard sounds in the distance ahead of me, and stopped abruptly. Too terrified to move, I waited fearfully for the noises to come again. I had not long to wait and my terror rose as I realised what the sounds were and where they came from. For what I could hear was singing, drunken, brawling singing, and in an instant my thoughts flew back to the men at the inn; the men I had seen in that long, low building playing skittles and drinking...and I remembered again the stories I had heard, stories of how dreadfully some of the miners abused their wives and families when they were drunk.

The singing sounded nearer now. My heart raced with fear... There was only one thing for me to do. I left the road and ran across the moor. As fast as I could, not looking to the right nor to the left, uncaring which way I was heading, I ran, stumbling and falling often, over the rough uneven ground. And I blessed the gathering gloom of night that had cloaked the moor like a mantle and hid me from their view. When the singing died away again into the distance, I stopped and began to make for the road again. Then it occurred to me that perhaps there were others following along the path. How could I be sure that I would not encounter more of them... It was clear that I must stick to the moor. I was so infinitely weary that all I wanted to do now was lie down and sleep but I knew that if I did I would die of cold.

I set off once more across the moor. How long I struggled on I have no sure way of knowing; it may have been for an hour or for more; but suddenly I heard another sound, the implications of which were almost as frightening as the drunken singing had been: it was the sea. There was no mistaking it. I stopped in consternation. If I could hear the sea I was heading in a completely wrong direction. I should have been going away from it... I was at a loss to know what to do. The roar of the waves sounded uncomfortably near. I must have walked round in a circle.

Desperately I tried to pinpoint the sound, to decide on which side of me the sea lay, but the howling wind seemed to be hurling the noise of the crashing waves from all directions. My hands and feet were numb with cold now and I knew that I must move on again. Slowly now and with infinite caution I set out again, mindful of the treacherous coastline towards which I could be heading, and then, oh, the blessed relief of it, I saw, way off in the distance, the faint glimmer of light... Almost weeping with joy I ran towards it. As I drew closer I could see that it was a large house towards which I was heading and in my heart I blessed whoever it was who had kept a light shining so late. Ornate iron gates loomed up in front of me. Summoning all my strength to make my icy fingers obey me, I struggled to open them. They were locked. With a despairing cry I seized hold of them and shook them for all I was worth. Somewhere a dog started howling; it sounded quite near. I prayed that somebody else might hear it and come out to investigate... Then my hands fell away from the cold, unyielding iron and I collapsed in a heap on the ground.

It was there that Nicholas Tangye found me. His expression on first seeing me was one of exasperated disbelief.

'No,' he said out aloud, bending over me and shining the lantern he carried full on my face. 'No, I do not believe it. Not *three* times in one day. It just cannot be.'

I was too exhausted to make any reply to him and just lay there, staring up at him helplessly. Then tears of relief and weakness started up in my eyes and began to roll down my cheeks. I let them fall, too weary to wipe them away.

I saw a look of compassion, quickly veiled, cross the good-looking face above me. 'What?' he asked. 'Tears from the spirited young lady of the coach...the young lady who can control her tongue.' It was the teasing, mocking manner of my former encounters with him back again, and it served to arouse me into making some effort at a semblance of dignity.

'I am extremely weary, sir,' I told him in a small voice. 'I am not in the habit of weeping at small discomforts I assure you, but tonight I have walked many miles and the cold is bitter...' My words trailed off as tears threatened to overcome me once more.

'Hush,' he commanded, and lifting me up in his arms, began to walk through the gates with me, calling to his dogs to follow him. He held me firmly yet gently and this time I made no protest.

'You seem,' he said, 'to have a habit of making a nuisance of yourself to me, young lady; and just how you came to arrive at my gates at this hour of the night is a story I would greatly like to hear—not now,' he silenced me as I opened my mouth to explain. 'In the meantime, the least I can do is to offer you shelter for the night.' We were going up a long winding drive as he spoke and rounding a bend I could see the outline of the house and lights breaking the darkness.

'You are very kind,' I murmured, my eyelids heavy, my voice drowsy, 'but I do not think I should presume—'

'Don't be such a damned little idiot,' he shouted down at me. 'Presume to do as you're told and be thankful.'

I said no more. My protest had been pathetically half-hearted in the first place. He needn't have shouted so rudely in order to gainsay me. I was more than ready to let him take command of the situation...I leaned my head against his shoulder and closed my eyes...

A round, motherly little woman helped me to bed. She took charge of me the minute that her master summoned her from her quarters and had me tucked in between sheets almost before I could realise what was happening to me. Her work-roughened hands were surprisingly gentle and her kindly eyes full of concern. Oddly enough, she showed no curiosity about me at all. I remember wondering vaguely if she were used to her master bringing strange women into the house in the middle of the night.

She kept up a volume of chatter and as

the endless stream of words rolled from her tongue, I sensed that she was trying to make me feel at ease, and silently blessed her for it. Much of what she said I failed to grasp, for apart from the fact that many of her words were dialect ones that I did not understand, my mind was refusing to register properly. Within minutes of my head touching the pillow I was fast asleep.

It was noon the next day when I awoke. At first I didn't know where I was. My mind still befogged by the mists of sleep I looked around me wonderingly. Then memory dawned and I sat up with a start. Of course! I was at the stranger's house. Nicholas Tangye's house! I must get dressed at once and see about making my way home again. It was then I think that the hopelessness of my position really hit me. Home, what home? I had none to go to. I sank back among the pillows again, a wave of despair engulfing me. No home, no money, no family; no-one to care whether I lived or died. No friends, for even this stranger who had shown me a kind of impatient kindness, could not be called a friend. There was, it seemed, but one course open to me.

I must return to the south coast and go into service at Tregonning Castle as his lordship had suggested.

I got out of bed and taking my purse from my cloak, counted out the meagre sum of money I still possessed. With a sigh of relief I saw that there was enough for the return coach journey. I dressed hurriedly, not knowing how far away I was from the inn where I would board the coach. There might be a long walk in front of me, and the sooner I started out, the better.

There was a knock on the bedroom door and the motherly figure of the previous night entered. 'So, you'm up my dear,' she greeted me with a smile. 'If you follow me to the breakfast room, mi dear, I'll be pleased to serve you with something.'

'Thank you,' I replied, 'but it is late and it is imperative that I continue on my journey just as soon as possible.'

The truth was that I did not wish to see Nicholas Tangye again. Although he had twice come to my aid, he had done so, if not in a grudging manner, at least in such a way as to make me feel a nuisance; and I did not wish to go through another encounter with him. Also I had a slight fear that he might start asking me questions about myself, questions that I had no wish to answer. After my high-flown remark in the coach about visiting Fistral Castle for 'personal and private reasons', it would be humiliating in the extreme to have to confess the truth of the matter...and I was uncomfortably conscious too of the way I looked, the travel-stained appearance of my clothes. Last night I had been too worn out to care, and in any case it had been dark, but this morning was a different matter...and especially so as I recalled his own impeccable attire in the coach.

But common courtesy demanded that I should thank him for my night's lodgings. I turned to the waiting housekeeper: 'Would it be possible for me to have a piece of paper and a pen?' I asked her. 'I wish to write a short note.'

She nodded and left the room to return two minutes later with what I had asked for. 'If you would be good enough to wait,' I asked.

I sat down at the dressing-table and wrote a brief letter of thanks, folded it, and took it across to the little housekeeper. 'Please give this letter to Mr Tangye after I have gone,' I told her. 'Now if you will show me the way to the entrance I am ready to leave.'

'Better eat,' she argued stolidly as she led the way along the landing. ' 'Tis cold out, and you be needing food, my dear, for your journey.'

I smiled and shook my head. We were about half way across the entrance when a door on the right was flung open. Nicholas Tangye stood there. He seemed taller than I had remembered and even more handsome. He was beside me in one powerful stride. 'Surely you are not leaving without taking breakfast,' he frowned, taking in at a glance the valise in my hand, my outdoor cloak. 'I am anxious to be getting on with my journey,' I replied hurriedly, not meeting his eyes.

'But a mere half-hour will make not the slightest difference, that is, unless you have some urgent appointment somewhere—?'

'No,' I interrupted hastily, alarmed at the trend the conversation was taking. 'I—I am in a hurry that is all. I am not in the least hungry—' My words tailed off before the look of disbelief on his face. I turned towards the front door, but gripping my shoulder hard he suddenly swung me round to face him.

'Of all the obstinate, proud little fools I have ever met,' he said impatiently, still holding my shoulder, 'you take the prize; you need some breakfast, it must be hours since you ate.' He let go of my shoulder, untied my cloak and with a determined grip of my arm led me into the breakfast room. He indicated a chair. I could see that it was useless to resist him further. 'Very well then,' I gave in, 'just a cup of coffee and then I will be off—'

'Cup of coffee bedamned,' he interrupted, 'you need something substantial inside you in this weather.' He crossed quickly to the sideboard returning with a steaming plate of bacon and eggs which he put down before me. 'Eat that,' he ordered.

I hesitated. I was hungry, but his high-handed behaviour annoyed me and filled me with resentment; the sooner I was out of his company the better. He must have seen my hesitation.

'You are a self-willed young lady,' he informed me, regarding me through narrowed eyes. 'But do you know, my dear Miss Pearce, displays of obstinacy such as yours tend to put me on my mettle.'

A pulse began to beat in my throat, something in his tone causing me apprehension. 'I do not understand you...' I began tremulously.

'You will,' he answered. He then walked away from me across to the window and stood looking out. Still with his back to me he said in a voice that was menacingly quiet: 'If you do not set about that food I have just offered you, Miss Pearce, of your own free will, I promise you that I myself will ram every mouthful of it forcibly down your slender white throat.'

Without a murmur I started to eat. I had not the slightest doubt that he meant what he said. He made no sign that he knew that I was obeying him but continued to stand over by the window, seemingly intent on the view. I was thankful that he did not turn, for I did not want him to see that I was hungry. Just how hungry I was in fact I had not realised until I started to eat. Sudden tears pricked my eyes, tears of thankfulness for his consideration.

I glanced across to where he was standing, at the broad powerful shoulders, the proud bearing. And as I ate I wondered what manner of man this Nicholas Tangye was, one minute so rude and arrogant, the next sensitive and perceptive to a degree. It came to me that in over-riding my wishes he had truly done me a service. Involuntarily my hand went to my throat, my 'slender, white throat...' I wondered if he realised that he had used those words. Somehow I did not think that he did. But consciously or not, he *had* used them, and I found them strangely pleasant. He turned from the window in the same instant that I rose from my chair.

'Thank you,' I said simply. 'That was delicious and I confess to being ready for it.'

With a typical gesture he waved my thanks aside. 'Coffee,' he insisted, going over to the sideboard. 'We shall now both take coffee.'

I walked across to where he himself had been standing in the curve of the window and looked out over the gardens. The breakfast room was obviously situated towards the back of the house for it was the kitchen gardens that met my eye. They did not look very attractive and had an air of neglect about them; inwardly

I contrasted them with the meticulously tended gardens at Tregonning Castle. But it was winter I reminded myself, no doubt they would look very differently in the spring.

Mr Tangye was coming over to me with the coffee. There was something about him that made me feel on edge. I would drink my coffee as quickly as I could and get on with my journey again. I was sure he was going to ask questions...

Sure enough as he handed me the delicate china cup he said: 'I have no wish to pry, Miss Pearce, but what are your plans? I seem to remember that in the coach you mentioned that you were on your way to Fistral Castle. Perhaps I may escort you there?' The one subject I had most dreaded!

'No!' The word came out more sharply than I intended. 'I mean,' I explained, choosing my words carefully so as to give no indication of my reception there, 'I have already been to Fistral Castle; my business there is finished. When you found me last night I was on my way back to the coaching inn.'

He was looking at me searchingly. 'But

you are nowhere near that inn,' he was clearly puzzled at my words. 'You are back on the coast, a bit further west than Fistral Castle assuredly but—'

'I got lost,' I interrupted him. 'I know that I took the right road for the inn initially, but—but—' I hesitated.

'Yes?'

'There were men coming towards me, drunken men, singing... I had seen them at the inn earlier in the day...I was afraid...'

'And so you ran across the moor. A dangerous thing to do, Miss Pearce. As a Cornishwoman you must have realised that.'

'I did,' I defended myself. 'But for me the drunken men held more terror than the moor; my grandmother told me about their doings many times.'

'Your grandmother? Not your mother?'

How quick he was to notice things. I hesitated before giving him an answer, unwilling to tell him the story my grandmother's letter had revealed to me. I would tell him just as much as courtesy demanded, nothing more. 'My mother is dead,' I told him flatly. 'And my father also. I never knew either of them. I was brought up by

66

my grandmother.'

Nicholas Tangye was regarding me thoughtfully, waiting, I sensed, for me to say more. When I did not do so he asked: 'And your grandmother, where is she now? I take it you wish to return to her?'

Tears brimmed over in my eyes and I felt them wet on my face. 'She, too, is dead,' I said sadly.

'You have other relatives?' His voice was unexpectedly gentle suddenly, and concerned.

Without a moment's hesitation I told him the truth: 'None,' I answered. 'I am completely alone in the world.'

'What will you do?' His tone this time was practical, incisive.

'There is but one thing I can do,' I replied. 'At least for the moment; and that is to go back to the south coast. Lord Tregonning told me that there was always a position for me at Tregonning Castle should I be in need of it, and since I have now neither home, money nor family, I do need it.'

'Tregonning, eh...my father, I believe, was acquainted with him. Spends a good deal of time abroad I fancy.'

'Yes,' I told him. 'That is so, but at the time of my grandmother's death, he was, fortunately for me, in England. You see,' I went on to explain, 'the cottage we lived in belonged to Lord Tregonning and was only a mile or so distant from the castle. His lordship was kind to me in my bereavement. I shall have a good place in his house and in any case there is no alternative.' I put down my coffee cup and began to do up my cloak once more. I held out my hand. 'Goodbye, Mr Tangye; once again my thanks for your hospitality, and now if you will be so good as to direct me back on to the road to the inn, I will take my leave of you.'

My outstretched hand was ignored. I looked up to find him regarding me keenly, a thoughtful look in his bold, blue eyes. My hand fell back to my side and I turned to go.

'One moment.' His words bit into the silence that had fallen between us. 'There *is* an alternative for you.'

I swung round. 'Yes? And what is that, Mr Tangye?'

'You could marry me,' he answered calmly.

CHAPTER 4

For seconds I was so dumbfounded that I couldn't speak. Then when the tumultuous beating of my heart died down a little and I regained some part of my composure, anger replaced my confusion. 'You mock me, sir,' I cried tersely. 'As I noticed in the coach, you appear to find amusement in causing discomfiture by your outrageous utterings; but I do not have to listen now, no longer am I a captive audience. Goodday to you.' I turned my back on him and began to walk hurriedly from the room.

In a flash he was in front of me, barring my path. He put a hand, gently this time, on my shoulder. Looking down at me he said quietly. 'Believe me, little one, I do not mock you. I have never been more serious in my life. I am asking you to be my wife.'

All at once the room seemed to be spinning around me. I put a hand to my brow and felt it cold and clammy; a wave of sickness swept over me and I think I should have swooned but for the protective arm which was swiftly placed around my waist. He led me to a sofa. 'Forgive me,' he murmured contritely. 'I had no idea my suggestion would give you such a shock. I am a man who makes up his mind about things in an instant, and I'm afraid I did not wait to consider the effect such behaviour might have—'

I stopped him by interrupting to ask if I could have a glass of water. He rose at once and went to the bell-rope. He refrained from talking any more until the servant had fetched the glass of water and withdrawn again. When I had recovered a little he took the glass from my hand and stood by the sofa looking down at me, a question in his eyes.

'Well?' he asked, briskly.

The water had refreshed me and I was myself again. 'Why do you wish to marry me, Mr Tangye?' I countered, with a briskness of tone equal to his. 'I am not so stupid as to imagine that you have fallen in love with me, nor do I think that you are the type of man to marry out of pity. It follows that you have an ulterior motive. I would like to know what it is.'

His response to my prim little speech

was a burst of hearty laughter. 'How right I was in thinking you had spirit,' he managed to say at last. 'How very right, by Gad!'

'I am waiting, sir,' I reminded him.

He stopped laughing and walked away from me, over to the windows again. His back towards me he stood silent for some minutes and then he began to speak. Still not looking at me, he said: 'There are several reasons why I have decided to marry you, Carenza. To enumerate: One: like many of our countrymen I am a bit superstitious. Now you have been thrown across my path three times in one day and I cannot believe that this is mere coincidence; it must have been ordained by the fates. Two: marriage to you would rid me of the tiresome female whom you have already met, who pursues me relentlessly—'

'Lady Penelope?' I interrupted.

'The same; a wife would be death to her scheming.'

'And the real reason, Mr Tangye, what is the *real* reason?'

He gave me a quick, enquiring glance.

'Come,' I continued, 'I am sufficiently intelligent to realise that the two reasons

71

you have stated are not the real ones; you say you are superstitious, and perhaps you are; but not, if I am any judge of character, not enough to let it affect major issues in your life; and as for ridding you of a scheming woman, I myself have seen that you are more than capable of dealing with any woman on earth—scheming or otherwise.'

A little aghast at myself for having been so outspoken I waited nervously for his reply to my outburst. I need not have worried. There was a gleam of approving amusement in Nicholas Tangye's eyes as he replied, 'I did not underestimate you, young lady. You are as discerning as I thought. Yes, there is another reason, the real one; come, I will show you.'

'Show me?' I echoed, mystified.

For answer he took me by the arm and led me out of the room. 'Follow me,' he ordered, and set off across the hall and up the wide shallow stairs. Greatly wondering, I followed.

At the end of a long, winding landing, he opened a door and stood back for me to precede him. As I went through the doorway, I gasped in astonishment, for there, inside what was obviously a nursery, was a small boy; an old nurse was with him. There was no need to ask who the boy was. He was the very living image of Nicholas Tangye himself. Confused and bewildered I turned to my host questioningly. Before I could speak he announced blandly:

'Before you accuse me of intent to commit bigamy, let me inform you that the child's mother is dead.' He was staring down at me, an unfathomable expression in his sea-blue eyes, I felt my face go hot, and I looked hurriedly away from him. The child meanwhile had stood, motionless, looking from one to the other of us, while the old nurse or whatever she was, beyond saying good morning, ignored us and continued her knitting.

'What is his name?' I asked.

'Piram.'

'Hello, Piram,' I said softly, and held out my hand. The child hesitated, took a step towards me, then ran across the room into a corner and began to weep quietly.

An expression that was a mixture of compassion and impatience covered his father's face and for a moment I thought he was about to scold the child, but he contented himself with glaring at the nurse and ordering her to stop knitting and attend to the boy. He did not speak again until we were back downstairs.

'Well?' he asked brusquely. 'You have seen the real reason. The boy needs a mother.'

'Yes,' I replied slowly, remembering the child's sad little face, the tragic, vulnerable air that hung over him. 'Yes, he certainly needs something...how long is it since...' I stopped, fearful of re-opening some wound of the past.

'Six months.' The reply was brusque, giving nothing away. 'It is six months since Piram's mother died. Since then,' he went on, 'there has been a succession of nurses, each one more stupid than the last, and each incapable of winning his confidence and affection.'

'How can you be sure that I could win his affection?'

'Because you already have a bond with the child,' the reply was swift, certain. 'He feels alone, bereft, so do you...you understand his problem because it is your own...'

'You may be right,' I told him thoughtfully. 'Perhaps I could help your little son and I am willing to try. But you do not have to marry me, Mr Tangye, I am willing to be employed by you as Piram's nurse.'

A closed, guarded look came over his face.

'As I have already told you,' he argued, 'there are other reasons why I have decided to marry you—reasons nonetheless valid for not being the most important; but putting all that aside, Piram needs a mother, not another nurse; he needs to feel secure; to know that the person to whom he gives his affection is going to be there always...if you were his nurse, the time would come when you would leave him...'

'There are other women who you could marry...indeed there might come a time when you might meet someone whom you could love.'

His answer was a mirthless laugh. 'There is little fear of that, I assure you, my dear girl. In my experience, love is a mythical state. I have little time for women and certainly would not dream of marrying again but for the boy. You, as I have just explained, already have an affinity with Piram, and coupled with the fact that I think you would annoy me slightly less than most of your sex, are the obvious choice for a mother. It would, of course,' he concluded, giving me a direct gaze which brought the colour rushing to my face, 'be a marriage in name only. I should make no demands upon you, of that you can be assured.'

Not looking at him I argued: 'But you know nothing about me, Mr Tangye—'

'I know as much as I need to do,' he interrupted. 'You need a home, the boy needs a mother; it's all perfectly simple.'

'To you perhaps, to me, no. I could not possibly enter into so serious a contract with someone who knows virtually nothing about me. When you know my history you may wish to withdraw your offer of marriage.'

'That I doubt very much,' came the reply, 'but if it will make you happier, all right, tell me what it is you feel I should know about you; in one so young and innocent-looking I cannot imagine there is a lurid, wicked past to be confessed.'

'Please do not mock me, sir,' I replied a little angrily. 'If you will do me the honour of taking me seriously in this matter, I will tell you my story.'

He was a good listener and did not once interrupt me as I told him about my life with my grandmother, her death, and my receiving the two letters from her. I showed him the one she had written to me. Only when I recounted what had taken place at Fistral Castle did he begin to ask questions.

'You say you know only the gist of what the letter to Sir Rupert Harford contained!' I nodded. 'And where is it now, let me see it.'

'But I no longer have it,' I told him. 'The Harfords kept the letter.'

'And the locket?'

'They kept that also.'

'What a silly child you are,' he said impatiently. 'Even if, as it would appear, your grandmother did make a mistake, the locket, since obviously it belongs now to you, should have been given back to you. I shall demand that they return it. They had not the slightest right to keep it.'

'You know the family then?'

'Yes, naturally I know them. They are neighbours. Not that I am at all enamoured of either of them, but that will not stop me from calling on them; we shall go together, after our marriage.'

'It does not trouble you then, the fact that I may have been born out of wedlock, that I do not know who my father was?'

'Not in the slightest,' he replied at once. 'I do not give a fig for convention or propriety. I am a law unto myself. I do precisely as I choose in all matters.'

'In that case...' I began hesitantly. I stopped. What was I about? How could I be so stupid as to be on the point of accepting this stranger's proposal of marriage? Such a thing was unthinkable! I must have let the man bewitch me. I threw back my head. 'I'm afraid, sir,' I said firmly, 'I must refuse your offer; I thank you for it, but no. When I marry, it must be for love.' I turned to go.

'Wait!' The word was a sharp command. 'Consider for a moment, my child, what love, as you call it, did for your mother, left to die among strangers, without a penny...and who knows what hardships she may have suffered before the oblivion of death brought blessed relief... Consider, little one, would not security have served her better than love? I am a rich man. Marry me and you will want for nothing...'

'Except love,' I interposed.

'You will have Piram's love, very soon, I am sure of it.'

'That, as you well know, was not the sort

78

of love I meant,' I replied slowly, 'precious though it would be...' I think then that he sensed I was weakening.

'Look,' he went on, 'I will leave you awhile until you reach a decision. In half an hour I shall return for your answer.'

Left alone I began to try to work out, as reasonably and objectively as I could under such circumstances, what I should do. It was a momentous decision that I was about to make; one that would affect my life irrevocably...my agitation and uncertainty were such that I could not sit still and I got up and began to pace the length of the room. Up and down, up and down; and as I walked I told myself that I was mad even to consider such an outrageous proposal. How could I marry a man who did not love me, I who had always dreamed of romance, of a grand passion and declarations of undying love from some handsome, god-like man who would worship me and whom I would worship in return... No, I could not, would not give up my dreams of such a union... I must marry for love... But whom?, argued the cold, hard voice of reason. As a servant in his lordship's castle what were my chances of meeting this idol?

And I forced myself to admit that the only people I would be likely to encounter in my lowly position, would be other servants and their like; good worthy men no doubt, and true, but not the princely figure of my dreams...and I remembered suddenly, a phrase from my grandmother's letter...the bit about my being different from her and her family, and of noble birth...and I knew swiftly and surely that I could never marry out of my own kind...that if I returned to the castle I would almost assuredly remain a maid for the rest of my life...It was not a pleasing prospect... And even if, I reasoned, by some remote chance I did meet some gentleman I could love, would he be likely to offer marriage to a bastard? might not my fate be the same as my mother's...

I pictured her, as Nicholas had already described her, dying a lonely death among strangers, a death brought about seemingly by love... Perhaps this strange person with whom I had been thrown into contact was right...perhaps love was after all, a mythical state; perhaps security was more worth seeking than love and devotion.

This man was offering me security, and strange and outrageous though much of his behaviour was, there was nonetheless much about him that was oddly pleasing to me... I thought of the boy—the little lost-looking boy and I remembered my own childhood. What would have become of me when fate flung my mother across their path if those goodly people had turned their backs...strangers, they had taken me in and loved me completely...to them I owed my life. Could I then not do what I was asked for this other motherless child? I knew that I must.

The half-hour was up. Nicholas returned to my side. 'I have decided,' I said slowly, 'to accept your proposal. I will marry you.' I looked up at him expectantly, awaiting his reply, but none was forthcoming. His only reaction was an enigmatic smile. 'Well,' I asked him, 'have you nothing to say?'

'What *is* there to say, little one? I have known all along that you would agree,' he said maddeningly.

'Oh,' I burst out, stamping my foot. 'You really are quite insufferable.'

'You'll get used to it,' he said calmly. 'Come, I will show you round the house and gardens.'

Trenance House, as I learned the house

was called, had been left to Nicholas by an uncle who had died childless.

'How long is it since you inherited?' I asked him.

'Twelve years ago,' came the reply. 'When I came of age. Yes,' he went on, an amused glint in his eyes, 'I am now thirty-three as you have already reckoned.' Vexed that my expression had given me away, I tried to regain my dignity by asking casually if Piram's mother had been Cornish, from a neighbouring family perhaps.....

'No.' The reply was curt. 'She was not.'

Stung by his tone I defended myself. 'Believe me, Mr Tangye, I do not wish to pry. I am not sufficiently interested in the matter to be truly curious. I asked merely out of politeness, I assure you.'

'Good,' he retorted at once. 'The less interest you show both in me and my affairs, my dear Carenza, the better our arrangement will be; confine your interest to the boy.'

'That is what I intend to do,' I replied swiftly.

As suddenly as it had come, his ill-humour seemed to vanish. He apologised for the neglected air of the house. 'Servants are somewhat of a problem,' he explained, 'and the house, as you see, is quite extensive.'

But not as extensive as either Tregonning Castle or Fistral Castle I thought to myself, both of which establishments had a well-maintained air with seemingly no lack of servants. Could it be that Nicholas Tangye had fallen on hard times perhaps? But he had told me he was rich. It was puzzling but I did not dare to question him about the matter.

We were leaving the house now and making our way towards the gardens at the front of the house. Like those I had observed from the breakfast room, they were rough and neglected.

'Someday,' he began, 'I intend to have the gardens landscaped. I want to be rid of these walls and have the whole lot thrown open; I was, in fact, on the point of having the work commenced when my wife...died.' There was a noticeable pause before the word died that struck me as being strange. I glanced up at him but his face gave nothing away. I murmured that I understood how such a terrible loss would naturally have driven all other matters into the background. He looked down into my upturned face, a brooding, unfathomable expression in his eyes.

'Yes,' he said vaguely. 'Yes indeed.' I received the distinct impression that he had not heard a word of what I had said, that at the mention of his wife's death his thoughts had flown back... I wondered how she had died. She must have been young, I thought to myself, like my own mother...

I realised he was speaking again, taking up the threads of his plans for the gardens, but I thought he seemed to have dragged himself back from the past with difficulty. His voice was flat and without enthusiasm as he continued: 'I intend to introduce exotic foreign plants and trees and have grottoes adorned with classical sculpture from Italy.'

'Have you visited Italy, Mr Tangye?'

The question was out before I could stop myself, but before he could answer I went on humbly, 'I beg your pardon; for one moment I had forgotten that I am not to show interest in your doings. Please ignore the question.'

An expression that was a mixture of amusement and annoyance crossed the handsome features. The amusement won and he laughed out loud. 'I'll say one thing for you, you waif-of-the-roads, you are not a bore. All the same,' he continued in sterner vein, 'please remember what I have said.' He took hold of my arm. 'Now I will show you the walk.'

The walk was planted with apple trees and was part of the gardens themselves. After we had walked the length of it, Nicholas led me towards the gates where he had found me the previous night. Turning to look back, I could see that the mansion and outbuildings were grouped round several courts, the outer one of which was entered beneath a gatehouse. It was an impressive picture and I remarked upon it.

Nicholas seemed pleased. 'It is right,' he said, 'that you should find your future home agreeable.'

My future home! The words leapt at me. What had I done? To what sort of life, what sort of man had I committed myself?

'Mr Tangye,' I said earnestly. 'Will you not please reconsider. Could I not remain here as Piram's nurse? Marriage is such an irrevocable step...'

I stopped in the face of the exhausted expression in his eyes. 'And how long do you think it would be before the Harfords had you hounded out of the district; Sir William is immensely powerful, and could, as he threatened, have you transported. As my wife you would have my protection. It is the only way.' He was striding quickly along as he talked and I had to run to keep pace with him. Neither of us spoke for some minutes.

We were heading towards the sea and nearing the cliff edge. When we reached it I looked down at the boiling sea and the foaming white spray. And in fancy I saw my mother, her long black hair spread out on the treacherous grey-green rocks. 'I will stay,' I said quietly.

We turned back then towards the mansion and as we walked Nicholas asked me if it had occurred to me what would have happened had I not collapsed at his gates. Until that very moment of his asking, it had not done so, but at once I saw his meaning and felt myself go cold at the thought.

'Yes,' he put it into words for me. 'A few more hundred yards and, short of a miracle happening, you would have walked over the cliffs to your death.'

I shuddered. 'From the sea and back to the sea,' I murmured. 'Perhaps it would have been better so—'

'Nonsense,' he interrupted sharply. 'Never let me hear you talk so again. You are young. Life is before you. Be thankful.'

Ashamed, I apologised. 'It was but a momentary thought. I did not mean it; it is just that I am weary and a little confused...'

I stumbled over a rough piece of ground and fell against him. He steadied me with a firm arm about my shoulders. 'You feel cold,' he announced abruptly. 'I was going to show you the deer park but it will have to wait. To walk another mile would be out of the question for you. We will return to the house at once. You must rest.'

I did not argue. The emotional and physical upheavals of the past forty-eight hours seemed suddenly to be taking their toll of me. I sorely needed both rest and quiet. Just before we reached the house Nicholas stopped and looked down at me.

'From the sea,' he murmured, 'from the sea. I like that. Some day I shall have you painted and call it "Girl from the Sea"!'

When we entered the house, Nicholas at once summoned the housekeeper. 'Take Miss Pearce to her room,' he commanded, 'and see to it that she has all she needs.'

He left me at the foot of the stairs. 'I suggest you have something to eat in your room and retire early,' he said kindly. 'I will see you in the morning.'

As I turned the corner of the stairs I looked down and he was still standing at the bottom, looking up at me. 'In case you really *are interested,*' he called after me. 'Yes, I have been to Italy.' With that he left me.

'He be a strange one, that,' muttered the little housekeeper. The remark, I felt, was made more to herself than to me and I did not reply. Inwardly I reflected that Nicholas Tangye was indeed strange. Strange and disturbing... I fell asleep wondering why he was so unwilling to talk about himself, and seeing again the look on his face when he had called me girl from the sea.

CHAPTER 5

That night I dreamed I was back in my grandmother's cottage. It was a dream so vivid and startlingly real that when I awoke the unfamiliar surroundings in which I found myself frightened me not a little. Then I remembered, but the remembrance did not comfort me at all; all it achieved was to change one form of fearfulness for another. Sadly I wondered what sort of life lay before me, a life without love or even hope of love... Then I fiercely reminded myself that at least I would have a name I could truly call my own, and the position of a lady. The way I had chosen must be far, far better than the only other course open to me, the life of a servant...

A knock on my door heralded the housekeeper; she had brought me morning tea. I thanked her, trying not to betray the fact that I was totally unused to such luxury. Looking back I do not imagine for one moment that she was deceived by my playacting, for as I was later to learn, she was not only kind, but also perceptive and shrewd. It brought home to me that morning an as yet unrealised complication of my position.

I mentioned the matter to Nicholas as soon as I got downstairs.

'I have up to now,' I told him anxiously, 'led an extremely simple life; I am not used to servants nor seeing to the running of a household such as this.'

'There is not the slightest need to be troubled on that account,' he answered. 'These things depend largely on using one's common sense—a virtue which you clearly possess. In any case,' he went on, 'if there is anything about which you are uncertain, leave the matter in Mrs Bray's hands.'

'The housekeeper?' It was the first time I had heard her mentioned by name.

'The same,' he smiled. 'She will be delighted to have her advice sought, I assure you.' A slightly mocking glint in his eyes, he added, 'Like most of her sex, she thrives on flattery.'

I bit back the quick retort that sprang to my lips at the faintly malicious jibe. Remembering his behaviour in the coach I knew he was deliberately trying to provoke me and so I refused to rise to the bait. As I had anticipated, he looked disappointed when I remained silent. It gave me a small feeling of elation to think that for once I had got the better of him.

'How soon can you be ready to go to Penzance?' The question startled me out of my reverie.

'Penzance?' I echoed stupidly. 'Why am I to go to Penzance?'

'To be married, of course,' he announced calmly, 'and to buy clothes. As my wife you will need to possess a wardrobe in keeping with your position.'

A wave of humiliation that I did not already have such clothes as were needed, swept over me. I could feel my cheeks burning as I insisted proudly that I already possessed one or two gowns of reasonable quality and had no wish for more.

'You will do as you are told,' he replied roundly. 'Nobody looks down on Nicholas Tangye or anything or anyone belonging to him. But it is not only for my sake that I insist; you will be able to hold your own with the Lady Penelopes of this world all that more easily if you can meet them on equal ground.'

I did not argue further. I still smarted a little from the slights I had received at that lady's hands. No doubt Nicholas knew what he was about.

It was decided that we should make the journey to Penzance in Nicholas's own carriage. I had never ridden in a private coach before in my life and felt a thrill of excitement when the ornate vehicle drew up outside the front entrance. It was not large, with room for four people inside, and was drawn by two splendid black horses. As we began our journey and Nicholas courteously arranged the cushions and rugs for my comfort, I knew a feeling of warmth and security such as I had not experienced since being left alone in the world. It was a feeling that was soon to be undermined.

Our route took us past the coaching-inn where I had alighted for Fistral Castle. As we approached it I mentioned to Nicholas that my trunk was still there.

'We will drive in then,' he announced, 'and I will make arrangements for it to be sent to Trenance House.'

While he was attending to the matter I decided to get down from the coach and stretch my legs. As I stood in the yard waiting for Nicholas I became conscious of curious glances cast in my direction by the landlord and his family and work-people. Because of my humble attire they probably thought me one of Nicholas's servants and I concluded that they were wondering at our presence at the inn together. A snatch of conversation that I caught confirmed the idea.

'I wonder how long this one will last?' I heard one of the girls ask with a giggle.

'No longer than the others,' came the instant reply. 'Not if she has any sense in her head, that is.'

It seemed clear that they had put me down as yet another nursemaid for Piram. I smiled to myself. What a surprise they would get if we called at the inn on our return journey, I mused, and they were to see my wedding ring.

Nicholas showed himself to be an excellent companion. He talked to me about many things during our journey and I was fascinated at the wideness of his knowledge. Not only was he extremely well informed, he was also witty and entertaining in his manner of conversing. He had travelled on the Continent a good deal it seemed and I was truly interested in his descriptions of the many places there that he had visited. Never once, however, did he make any reference to his first wife and I knew better than to ask him about her.

During a lull in the conversation I fell to thinking about what the girls at the inn had said. With an unpleasant start, it suddenly occurred to me that there could have been other meanings to their words. I looked across at Nicholas, young, handsome, rich...could it be that they thought I was his mistress...that there had been others...the thought was wholly distasteful to me. The glow of warmth and security left me. I remembered what Nicholas had said earlier about having little time for women. Perhaps he had time for them in one respect! Unaware that I was being observed I let a smile of disdain curve my lips.

'Something amuses yet displeases you at the same time?' The remark was more statement than question.

'Yes,' I said evenly. 'Something does.'

Nicholas continued to regard me carefully for a moment, but made no further comment.

Choosing clothes in Penzance was exciting. Never in my life before had I experienced anything like it, for what few gowns I had had in the past had been made either by my grandmother or myself. I could hardly believe my eyes when I saw the dazzling array of fashions set out for my appraisal, and I am quite sure that if I had been on my own I should never have made up my mind which ones to buy. But Nicholas decided which ones would suit me and made his choice instantly. I was relieved that on this occasion he informed the vendeuse who attended us, that he and I were to be married: it saved me from feelings of embarrassment and from speculating glances.

When he was asked where the clothes were to be sent, Nicholas announced that they must be delivered that day to an inn, the White Hart. Outside again, he explained to me: 'I have stayed there on one or two occasions in the past and have found it convenient; the food is palatable and the surroundings reasonably agreeable.'

Sure enough the inn was clean and comfortable. My room was small but pleasant and overlooked the sea. When the packages arrived I was tempted to open them all out and look at the fascinating silks and velvets all over again, but contented myself with unpacking only one, a turquoise velvet, my favourite of the whole collection. On impulse I decided to put it on. I was just swirling around in it happily when there was a knock on my door. I ran to open it. There on the threshold stood Nicholas. A look of admiration, quickly veiled, passed over his face.

'It would be unwise to wear that dress here, my dear child,' he said seriously. 'Take if off and change before you come down for supper.'

I did as I was bid and packed the dress away again, and clad once more in my serviceable travelling apparel joined Nicholas for our meal. There were several rough-looking men sitting about drinking and they eyed us appraisingly as we ate. The food, as Nicholas had said, was palatable. Afterward Nicholas went with me as far as the door of my room. 'Good night, Carenza,' he said. 'Be sure to bolt your door.' I nodded. I had already decided to do so of my own accord.

Later that night I was awakened by the sound of voices outside in the road below my window. I got out of bed and peered out into the darkness through the small panes of glass. It was very dark, with no moon or stars and I could not see clearly at all, but I was able to make out a small group of men, three or four at the most, talking earnestly together immediately below me. Suddenly one of them raised his voice.

'It be risky,' he was saying, 'women be clever at getting things out of a man—'

'I tell 'ee Mr Tangye says she knows nothing,' interrupted another one, 'and he'll see that she never does.'

Their voices sank to whispers again and I heard no more. Puzzled and a little frightened I got back into bed. It was some time before I slept again.

We were married just as soon as the necessary arrangements could be made; two men I had seen at the inn, and who were apparently known to Nicholas, acted as witnesses. I decided to wear the turquoise velvet dress and the plumed hat which had been chosen to go with it, for the ceremony. Strangely enough, I did not feel nervous. All during the time leading up to the moment of entering the church, I had been a bundle of nerves, and unable to eat hardly at all, but standing beside Nicholas at the altar I experienced a feeling of serenity such as I had never known. Although the decision to marry him had been forced upon me by what seemed a series of cruel blows from fate, and although that decision had seemed, when I made it, nothing more than the lesser between two evils, I had a feeling of *rightness* about it that was strong and unmistakable.

Maybe the beauty of the church and the dignity of the words we were repeating were in some way the cause, I do not know, but it seemed to me as I stood there and held out my hand for Nicholas to place the ring on my finger, that I was in my rightful place...that all my life had been but a prelude to this one moment...that it had been ordained...and the feeling was all the more breathtaking perhaps because of its being so totally unexpected...my hand trembling a little I looked up into Nicholas's face and surprised an expression that made my heart beat faster... Mentally I shook myself. This was to be a marriage of convenience, a marriage in name only... I must indeed be becoming fanciful to have imagined a hint of passion in the sea-blue eyes... Once more I looked up at him, the man who was now my husband. His face wore an expression that was cool and impassive, which was, I told myself impatiently, just as it should be and how I wished it to be.

But no matter how firmly I reminded myself of this; I did not succeed in erasing the faint stirrings of an ache that had unaccountably begun to gnaw at my heart. I was relieved to be out of the church and into an atmosphere more mundane and less conducive to fanciful daydreams...

Back at the inn we enjoyed a modest wedding breakfast, joined once more by the two witnesses. When it was over I went up to my room to change into my travelling apparel ready for the journey back to Trenance House. As I came downstairs I saw that the two witnesses had gone and that Nicholas was deep in conversation with two other men in the doorway of the room. So earnestly were they talking together that I do not think they heard my approach. With something of a shock, I recognised one of the men's voices: it was one of those that I had heard beneath my window in the night. Looking up suddenly, Nicholas saw me and made his way towards me. The two men left and we made our way to the waiting coach.

As we began our journey I kept wondering about the dark, swarthy-looking men. Strange companions for a man like Nicholas to have, I reasoned. I wondered if I dare ask him about them and had almost plucked up courage to do so when I recalled his admonition not to pry into his affairs. Better not to displease him, I concluded, but it did not stop me from speculating...the men in question were unmistakably sea men...fishermen. I could tell not only from their clothes but also from their eyes...eyes that seemed always to be searching the horizon. Could it be that Nicholas was involved in some smuggling activity with them? It seemed to me highly possible. After all, had he not told me himself that he did precisely as he liked in all matters? That he was a law unto himself? And was not smuggling just the sort of hair-raising dangerous adventure that would appeal to his devil-may-care temperament?

'You look thoughtful and unduly serious. Does the fact of being married to me weigh so heavily upon you already?' Nicholas's question put an end to my reverie. I blushed and did not look at him as I answered:

'I was not thinking about marriage at all.'

'But you were thinking about me. Come, do not deny it, your expression betrayed the fact. You were looking at me in what can only be described as a speculative manner.'

I blushed even more hotly beneath the teasing banter, the amusement in his eyes. 'I—I was only wondering what sort of pastimes you found agreeable,' I stammered, 'if...if you liked sailing for instance...' My words trailed off before the unbelieving look in his eyes.

'I have a feeling you are dissembling with me a trifle,' he remarked. 'But we will let it pass. It is of no consequence to me really.' We lapsed into silence. An unreasonable chagrin that my opinion of him should matter so little, welled up in my heart.

To my delight, Nicholas decided that we should call once more at the coaching-inn; partly, he said, so that he could make sure that my trunk had been despatched and also to take refreshment. In the cobbled yard when we arrived was the most cumbrous-looking vehicle imaginable, I recognised it as the stage-wagon. It was arched over with a canvas roof and the wheels were of enormous breadth. Nicholas explained that this was to prevent them sinking in the mud. When the wagon set off again the neck-bells worn by the eight large horses pulling it, made the most delightful tinkling sound. The driver, clad in a coarse linen smock, raised his long whip in greeting to us as he passed by. It was by far the longest whip I had ever seen and must have been as tall again as the man himself. When I commented on this, Nicholas smiled and told me that in spite of its formidable appearance, the whip was seldom used as horses were never driven at more than a walking-pace. 'In fact,' he went on, 'it takes three weeks to journey from Falmouth to London in that thing, I'm told.'

We were not the only ones watching the wagon's departure. Many of the inn staff were there, including the two women I had heard gossiping on our outward journey. Seizing the opportunity thus offered, I pulled off my expensive new gloves and made a great display of fixing my hat more securely, displaying my hands, particularly my left one, as much as possible. They could not fail to notice my wedding ring, and their looks of surprise when they saw it, filled me with quiet satisfaction. That, I reasoned, should put a stop to their wagging tongues whether they thought me nursemaid or mistress... My satisfaction would have been short-lived however, had I known precisely why the women looked so surprised. But I did not know, and it was some time before I was to find out...

During the remainder of the journey Nicholas seemed irritable. He answered me curtly, when I made an attempt at conversation and a moody, almost savage expression covered his face. He must have read the look of dismay in my eyes, for he suddenly leaned forward and with a completely different tone said: 'Forgive me, child. I am an ill-tempered brute, not worthy of such a gentle companion.' He patted my arm with a fatherly gesture. I smiled back, happier suddenly. The feeling did not last long...

We arrived home to find Lady Penelope awaiting us. Nicholas swore roundly when Mrs Bray met us in the hall with the information. 'That woman!' he fumed. 'Now how the devil did she know when we were expected back?' He turned back to the servant. 'Where is she?'

'In the drawing-room, sir.' Nicholas looked at me.

'There is no escape,' he shrugged. 'We shall have to put in an appearance.' As we went towards the drawing-room he bent down and whispered: 'Leave it to me. I am fairly adept at getting rid of people. I have no wish to receive, even Lady Penelope, and the shock of hearing that I am married should shake her self-possession somewhat and render her less persistent.'

But Nicholas had underestimated the beautiful Penelope. She sailed across the drawing-room, arms outstretched in welcome the moment we entered, and with a dazzling smile offered her congratulations to us both. Nicholas was clearly stunned.

'Now how the blazes—' he began.

Penelope held up a slender, exquisitely-ringed hand. 'How did I know you were married?' she teased good-humouredly. 'That is what you were about to ask was it not, Nicholas? Well, let me tell you. The day you left for Penzance I was out riding on the moor and I met your groom. I recognised the horse he was riding as one of yours. I was on my way to see Lady Treglown and as I was not too sure of the way I called to your groom and asked him. In the course of the conversation,' she went on, 'he told me that you and Miss Pearce had gone to Penzance to be married—'

'And also the day we were due to return?' interrupted Nicholas with a faintly malicious smile.

'Oh, I found that out from Mrs Bray,' replied Lady Penelope shamelessly. 'After all, I felt that someone of your own class should be here to welcome you and as you are so new to the district and acquainted with but a few of us I regarded it as my duty to be here.'

'Indeed,' murmured Nicholas, and I suppressed the small smile which came to my lips. For once, I thought to myself, he has had the wind taken out of his sails completely, and although I did not like Lady Penelope, I could not help admiring her style and panache. I turned towards her with a smile.

'It was most kind of you to come,' I told her. 'Perhaps you will do us the honour of taking tea with us?'

There was not the slightest hint of condescension in her voice as she replied that she would be very happy to do so. 'You in turn must come and visit with me,' she enthused. 'I shall be delighted to welcome you at Harris Point as soon as possible.'

All through tea she behaved in this same gracious and charming manner towards me and I concluded wryly, that marriage to Nicholas had made me socially acceptable in her eyes. In the coach on our first meeting I had been a nobody, quite beneath her notice. Now as Mrs Nicholas Tangye, I was somebody. Somebody worth knowing and cultivating. How silly it all is, I thought to myself, for I am precisely the same person now, as I was then, no worse, no better. But I decided that it would be both childish and stupid to hold her former attitude towards me against her; obviously she now wished to be friendly and I was ready to comply with that wish. From the sardonic look in Nicholas's eyes I deduced that he had reached precisely the same conclusions as I had myself and that he was cynically amused at Lady Penelope's transparency.

Just before she left us, Nicholas went out of the room for a couple of minutes and the two of us were alone together. Immediately, the smile left her face.

'No doubt you think you've been very clever,' she hissed. 'But you may have landed yourself with much more than you bargained for, *Mrs* Tangye.' There was a wealth of sarcasm in her voice as she spoke my married name.

'What on earth are you suggesting?' I cried out in alarm. 'What do you mean, Lady Penelope?'

She hesitated a second before replying, a

cold, calculating air about her. 'There are rumours,' she began, 'that—' She broke off as the door opened and Nicholas returned. 'I really must go now,' Lady Penelope, her face wreathed in smiles once more, rose to take her leave.

Nicholas looked at me closely as he accompanied her to the door. 'Are you all right,' he asked suddenly. 'Her ladyship didn't say anything to upset you while I was absent, did she?'

'Yes,' I replied slowly. 'She did. She hinted that I was courting disaster of some kind by marrying you—'

'Jealousy,' he interrupted. 'She is deliberately trying to upset you, as I expected she would. Pay not the slightest attention to her.' He looked at me anxiously. 'You did not believe her...?'

'I'm tired,' was the only reply I made. 'If you have no objections I will go to my room now.'

'Just as you wish,' he agreed. 'But remember what I have said. Dismiss the matter from your mind.'

Resolutely I tried my best to do so. But as I lay in my bed that night, alone and besieged with nameless fears and doubts, I realised that Lady Penelope's words had hit me hard. I made up my mind to get in touch with her the very next day and demand that she tell me what she had been hinting at. And I faced the fact that it was not only Lady Penelope's innuendo that had upset me, but also something about Nicholas's reaction...he had been, I thought, unduly insistent that I pay no heed, too insistent perhaps...

CHAPTER 6

Next morning I asked Nicholas if he had any objections to my taking a drive over the moors. He seemed surprised, but also, I thought, in some way relieved.

'Go by all means,' he acquiesced pleasantly. 'I suggest you order the small carriage to be brought round. Young Bray, the groom will drive you.'

I wondered what his reaction would have been could he have divined my real intention that morning, which was to drive to Lady Penelope's residence. We were having breakfast together for the first time and I got the impression that Nicholas found the occasion almost as awkward and disconcerting as I did, and was glad of a mundane topic of conversation.

Only when he was leaving the breakfast-room did he bring up a more personal matter. 'Did you remember to unlock the communicating door before you left your room?' he enquired, from a step behind me.

'Yes,' I answered, colour mounting my cheeks in my embarrassment. I walked hurriedly away from him, glad that he could not see my face.

He had explained the matter the previous night, our first night at Trenance House as man and wife. 'It is essential,' he had told me, 'that we occupy this suite with the communicating door between the bedrooms, otherwise the servants will gossip. For my own part I do not care a fig what anyone, servant or otherwise, cares to conclude, but for your sake I think it would be unwise to ask for comment by sleeping in different parts of the house. You can lock the door every night,' he had gone on, a slightly teasing look in his eyes, 'but you must remember to open it each morning when I am safely up and out of the way of course,' he concluded with a wicked grin.

Not meeting his eyes, I had agreed that it seemed the most sensible thing to do under the circumstances.

From the breakfast-room I went to the nursery in search of the little Piram. I had decided that it was best to waste no time at all in trying to win his confidence. I hoped, too, to win his love, but this I knew would not be easy and would take time. As the child was only three years old, Nicholas had decided that he was too young for any explanations about my presence. I was to be there, that was all.

We hoped and prayed that he would grow to accept me as someone who loved him and would not go away from him.

The nurse greeted me in surly fashion and I sensed immediately that she resented me. I decided to ignore her churlishness and outlined, in what I hoped was a pleasant but firm manner, what I had come to arrange.

'From now on,' I told her, 'you will consult me on all matters regarding Piram. Both Mr Tangye and I are agreed upon this.' She made no answer. 'Furthermore,' I went on doggedly, 'I intend to spend as much of my time as possible with the child myself; it will mean, of course, that you yourself will be able to have more free time.' I looked at the old wrinkled face expectantly as I spoke, but all she said was:

'I have all the free time I want.' The words were muttered in the rolling vowels of her native Cornish and accompanied by an insolent stare. I was at a loss to know how to deal with the woman. Inwardly I was a trifle frightened of her, but did my best to hide the fact. There was something almost witch-like about her, and I began to understand something of the difficulties which must have confronted Nicholas left with a small, motherless child. He must have been desperately in need of a nurse to have even considered this one.

I wondered what the other servants made of her. It struck me then that I had seen no other servants, only Mrs Bray. Could it be that these two women, neither of them young, made up the entire staff? It was unthinkable in so large a house. And why had not Nicholas mentioned the fact when I had voiced my doubts about handling servants... Aware that the old sloven was staring at me I turned my attention to the child who had been eyeing me solemnly the while.

'Hullo, Piram,' I said gently. 'How would you like to come for a ride in the carriage with me?'

' 'Tis too cold.' The old woman's tone was defiant.

'Nonsense,' I replied a great deal more confidently than I felt. 'If the child would like to come, he may do so. The cold will not hurt him at all if he is warmly wrapped. Would you like to ride over the moor, Piram?' I smiled down at him as I spoke, but there was no answering smile in the sad little face. He remained silent, looking at me cautiously. Suddenly I made up my mind.

'He shall come,' I told the old woman authoritatively. 'Have him dressed and ready for me in half-an-hour if you please.'

For a moment I thought she was going to defy me but she must have decided against such a course, and contented herself with muttering, ' 'Tis too cold,' once more.

Outside in the corridor I drew a deep breath of relief. The old woman had, I reckoned, realised that the mistress of Trenance House intended to be obeyed. I fervently hoped that I should have no further trouble with her. I put my head round the nursery door again. 'I shall

112

expect you to come along as well,' I told her and withdrew without giving her chance to answer me.

Once away from the house, I instructed the groom to drive to Harris Point, and asked him how far it was.

'Five or six mile et be,' he answered, and added that although the house was on the coast, the road to it wound inland for part of the way.

As we journeyed over the moors I studied the face of the child sitting opposite me. There was something there that wrung my heart and I determined to do my uttermost to take away the lost, bewildered expression from the tragic little face. Every time I caught him looking at me, I smiled reassuringly in an effort to make him feel at ease with me. I tried to make conversation with the old Mrs Polglaze, as I had learned she was called but as she answered only in monosyllables I soon gave up, and I began to regret having brought her along; something told me that I should have made more headway with Piram had I had him to myself.

The journey was nearing its close and we were winding our way back to the sea.

'How much further now?' I shouted to the groom.

'Two more miles it be,' he answered.

I was pleased to notice that a flicker of interest appeared in Piram's eyes as soon as we caught sight of the sea.

'Do you like the water, Piram?' I asked quietly. The child nodded.

'So do I,' I responded quickly. 'When it is warm again we will go there together; would you like that?' Again the child nodded. I felt a flicker of hope. A link had been established between us.

Harris Point, like Fistral Castle, stood on a promontory jutting out to sea. It was a house roughly on the same lines as Trenance House but smaller. As we approached the inner courtyard, my heart began to beat nervously. I wanted to know what Lady Penelope had meant, and yet at the same time I dreaded to hear, lest the knowledge be more devastating than the suspense.

I did not leave the coach but sent the young Bray to the house to ask if Lady Penelope was at home. He was back in seconds with the news that very early that morning her ladyship had gone away and would not be back for two weeks. I could have wept with frustration. Two whole weeks before I could find out what she had been getting at.

Yet as we began the homeward journey there was a feeling of relief mingled with my emotions... It was almost like being granted a reprieve, but from what I did not know... I began to feel unaccountably optimistic. Perhaps Lady Penelope had just been trying to upset me, for after all hadn't Nicholas said she was pursuing him? No doubt she was jealous of what she imagined to be between Nicholas and myself. So I reasoned and argued in my mind, bolstering myself up. I would dismiss the matter from my thoughts completely and concentrate on my duty. The little Piram should have my whole, undivided attention.

So wrapped up had I been in my thoughts that I had not noticed the black clouds that had come rolling in from the west. The rain, when it began to beat down on the carriage roof, startled me not a little. We were on the open moor at the time and there was nowhere where we could shelter. I urged the groom to bring the horses to a standstill and to come and shelter inside the coach but he wouldn't hear of such a thing. Instead he drove the horses faster than ever and we lurched and bumped over the uneven track at what seemed to me an alarming rate. I lifted Piram away from the nurse and sat him beside me, putting my arm about his thin little shoulders.

Suddenly there was a shout and the carriage ground and slithered to a halt. 'What is it?' I called out, slightly alarmed.

Young Bray appeared at the window. 'Somebody be out there,' he shouted, 'on the moor. She'm running towards the carriage.'

I peered out through the streaming windows and gasped in astonishment at the sight that met my eyes: a woman, her sodden garments wrapped round her like a shroud, her long grey hair plastered about her head and shoulders, was heading frantically towards us.

'Open the door,' I called.

The groom did as he was bid and the woman leapt into the carriage. Piram at once began to whimper but I held him closer and whispered that everything was all right. The woman, without uttering a word, had planted herself beside the old Mrs Polglaze who edged away from the dishevelled figure with alacrity, muttering under her breath furiously the while.

There was something about the stranger that was vaguely familiar...she was gazing about her complacently as if being soaked to the skin and taking a flying leap into a passing carriage were in no way extraordinary to her. I wished her good-day and asked if she had been out in the deluge for very long.

She appeared not to hear me and made no answer. She was staring at me now in the most disconcerting way... I looked away from her, away from those strange looking, sad eyes...and memory came flooding back to me. Those were the eyes I had seen through the carved balustrade of the minstrel's gallery in Fistral Castle—the wild eyes that had seemed to burn in the pale ghostly face that had watched silently.

'I've seen you,' she announced suddenly, in a voice that was surprisingly cultured. I looked up in amazement, her eyes now were calmer, with less remoteness about them.

'Yes,' I replied, by now extremely curious about my strange companion. 'Yes indeed. I came to Fistral Castle some time ago and you saw me there, I believe.'

She nodded. 'Are you coming back?' she asked after a minute or two.

'No,' I told her. 'I have no more business at Fistral Castle. But let me introduce myself properly. I am Carenza Tangye, Mrs Nicholas Tangye of Trenance House.' I held out my hand and she touched it lightly with her own, withdrawing it quickly and pushing it back inside her wet cloak. But she wasn't quite quick enough. I saw that her hand was torn and bleeding. 'You are hurt,' I cried. 'Your hand is cut and needs attention; we must take you at once to your home—'

'No!' The cry was sharp, emphatic. A look of fear came over her features.

'Then perhaps you will come home with me to Trenance House,' I suggested, 'and have your wounds attended to there—'

'No!' she cried out again. 'No!'

I did not know what to say to her next. She kept her hand hidden in the folds of her long grey cloak as if defying me to mention the matter again. Suddenly she leaned towards me. 'You won't tell them, will you?' she whispered.

'Tell whom?' I asked her, greatly puzzled. 'Tell whom, and what—'

'Them,' she interrupted. 'They don't know you see.'

Her eyes were wild again and she seemed now to be staring right through me... I began to feel frightened. Instinctively my arm tightened about the boy. I decided I had better shout for the groom to stop the carriage and send this odd woman about her business...the storm was dying out and in any case she was wet through already.

As if anticipating my action, the stranger suddenly sprang towards the door. 'Wait,' I cried. 'Wait. You will harm yourself. I will tell the coachman to stop.'

The moment the carriage halted, the woman flung open the door and threw herself to the ground.

'No, don't get down,' I called up to the groom. 'Our passenger is leaving us that is all.' I turned back to her. 'Are you all right?' I asked anxiously. For answer she got to her feet and one hand holding open the carriage door, thrust her head inside once more.

'Why don't you come back?' she asked, and her voice this time was gently chiding and her expression sane.

'What do you mean?' I asked in

amazement. But the mad look returned to her eyes and she stared at me vacantly. I had had enough of her. 'We must go now,' I said. 'If you will be good enough to close the door—' I stopped. Mrs Polglaze was heaving herself up from her seat. With one almighty pull she wrenched the door from the woman's grasp and slammed it in her face, calling up to the groom at the same time, to drive on.

'You need not have been so rough with her,' I upbraided the old nurse indignantly. 'The poor creature needs our pity and—'

'Mad,' she interrupted me. 'She'm mad, should be bowssened.' And there was fear in her marble-black eyes.

As the horses set off again, I turned and looked back. The woman was standing where we had left her, staring after us. And then she laughed, laughed with that same inhuman cackle I had heard at Fistral Castle.

When later I recounted the episode to Nicholas he did not appear impressed.

'That would certainly be the "mad aunt" of the Harfords,' he confirmed. 'She is said to be in the habit of roaming over the moor in all weathers. She's harmless, of course; you had no need to be frightened of her.'

'Mrs Polglaze looked afraid,' I defended myself. 'She said the woman ought to be bowssened, whatever that means.'

Nicholas at once explained. If a lunatic was bowssened it meant that he was pushed backwards into a pool or pond and then tossed up and down in the water by a strong fellow provided for the purpose; when the victim, through weakness, lost some of his fury he was conveyed to church where certain masses were sung over him; if his wits returned, thanks were offered, if not, the bowssening was repeated again and again while there remained any hope of life for recovery.

'Who could behave in such a cruel way?' I cried, aghast at such a story. Nicholas smiled grimly. 'Plenty of people, I assure you, it is quite staggering, the inhumanity of man to his fellows when confronted with something which he fears and does not understand.' I gave a shudder.

'That laugh the poor creature makes is a spine-chilling sound,' I told him, 'I seem as though I can still hear it.'

'No doubt its effect would be heightened by the wind and the rain,' Nicholas smiled. 'On a mist-shrouded moor one's imagination can easily run riot. As I have told you, the woman is harmless even though she is a little deranged.'

More than a little deranged, I thought to myself, as lying in bed later that same night I had difficulty in ridding myself of the memory of the poor, demented creature. And I kept recalling her parting question:

'Why don't you come back?'

Could it be that she just wanted me to visit the castle again because she liked visitors to come, or could it be that she believed I was someone else. It was all very puzzling and confusing but I decided that it was possible that the latter explanation was the true one, for in that one brief moment of asking the question she had seemed sane. I wondered if I would ever encounter her again, ever discover what she really did mean...

I turned over in the four-poster bed and composed myself for sleep. Just before I slept I realised with some surprise that I had given no thought whatever to Lady Penelope and her suggestions. The 'mad woman' as I had privately christened her, had driven the matter completely out of my head; for that I was grateful to her.

CHAPTER 7

But during the next few days all thoughts of the mad woman herself were driven out of my mind by something which happened within Trenance House itself; Piram became ill, very ill.

On the third day after our journey to Harris Point he started with a feverish cold which grew quickly and progressively worse. The old nurse announced in no uncertain terms that he had caught cold by going out in the carriage; had she not told me that the weather was too cold, not once, but twice. Her manner was more insolent than ever and although to be fair to her she may have been sorry that the child was ill, I am certain that she was gratified at a turn of events which seemed to lend credence to what she had stated. I myself was frantically worried about the child and suffered at the thought that perhaps Mrs Polglaze was right. But Nicholas, to my relief, dismissed the idea as nonsense.

'The child has travelled in cold weather before,' he argued, 'and on longer journeys by far, without suffering any ill effects. You must not blame yourself, Carenza. The child has caught some malady, but it is no fault of yours or anyone else's.' He was bending over the flushed child as he spoke, his expression one of great anxiety. He looked up at me across the narrow bed.

'You will stay beside him until I return with a doctor.' It was neither question nor order; just a statement of fact and as such it needed no answer.

It seemed an eternity before I heard the sound of horses' hooves outside in the courtyard and knew that Nicholas was back again. I tiptoed to the nursery window to see him dismounting and with him a small dapper-looking man I presumed to be the doctor. They wasted no time in coming upstairs.

I was sure that Piram was worse; in the hours that had elapsed since Nicholas had set out, his temperature had, I felt sure, soared alarmingly. Anxiously I hovered behind the two men as the doctor examined the child. The diagnosis did not take long. Straightening up, the doctor turned to Nicholas and me and announced: 'Measles.' He pointed out the tell-tale rash which was just beginning to appear beneath the surface of the skin behind the child's ears.

I listened carefully to his instructions as to how the child was to be nursed. Mrs Polglaze, knitting in a corner of the nursery, was listening too. She was eyeing the doctor with ill concealed animosity and I wondered what thoughts were going on in the old woman's mind. It seemed clear that she had a poor opinion both of the doctor and his instructions.

I asked if I should sleep in the child's room but the doctor was against the idea. 'You are very young,' he argued. 'And it is possible you may catch the disease. It will suffice if you look in on the child once or twice; the old nurse, unless I am mistaken, will insist on remaining in the room and she can call you if alarmed.'

True enough, Mrs Polglaze did as the doctor had prophesied. She had had the measles, she argued, many years ago and had no fears of catching it again. And she went on to suggest that it might be better if I didn't go near Piram at all: it was better not to take risks. Let her nurse the child to health again: she knew all about the measles.

Nicholas was at first inclined to agree with her but I would not hear of such a thing. 'I will obey the doctor and not sleep in Piram's room,' I conceded. 'But I shall watch over him during the day time, I insist upon it. I am not in the least afraid of catching the disease; I would not dream of denying the child my attentions and help.'

So Nicholas gave in to me and I had a feeling that he was pleased by my reaction; the thought in turn, pleased me.

When the time came for me to leave Piram and retire to my own room, I thought he still looked very ill, but certainly no worse than he had done during the day. I had done all that the doctor had told me and had been careful to follow his instructions implicitly. Mrs Polglaze had watched my ministrations in silent disapproval, and seemed impatient to be rid of me. I was reluctant about leaving the child in her care and before I did so, emphasised repeatedly that she was to come for me at the smallest sign of deterioration in Piram's condition. She nodded irritably, a gleam of something I could not fathom in her face and closed the door behind me with unflattering haste.

The stillness of night descended on the house. There wasn't a sound and I ought to have dropped off to sleep the minute I got into bed, for worried though I was about Piram, I was so tired that it seemed even such great anxiety as I felt could not keep me awake. But I was wrong. Perhaps I was too tired to sleep—I had often heard my grandmother say that this was possible—I do not know, but whatever the cause, sleep eluded me. In the light of the events of that night, I now believe it was some inner sixth sense that kept me wakeful until the small hours...

It was just after I had heard the grandfather clock in the entrance hall striking two that I first heard the sound that jerked me bolt upright in my bed. It was a curious croaking sound and accompanied by something that sounded like the whirring of a bird's wings.

Deeply puzzled, and a little afraid, I got out of bed and crept to the door which opened onto the landing...cautiously and as silently as I could I inched the door ajar...there was no mistaking where the strange sounds were coming from...it was from Piram's room. Without pausing to put on a wrap I ran across the landing in my nightgown and down the corridor towards the child's room. The noises were louder now but I still could not make out what they were. Anxious not to wake Piram should he still be sleeping in spite of the noises, I quietly pushed open his bedroom door... Never until I die shall I forget the sight that greeted my eyes.

Hanging from one of the beams in the ceiling was a live fowl. And as it writhed and flapped in agony, the old nurse bent over it, plucking at it with bent and claw-like fingers to wrench the feathers from its scrawny body. The grisly business had obviously been going on for some minutes for the fowl was almost plucked clean and its croaks and squawks of pain growing feebler every second.

'Mrs Polglaze,' I shouted angrily, running into the room. 'Whatever are you doing? Have you taken leave of your senses?'

I tried to pull her away from her horrible task, but she pushed me off.

' 'Twill cure the boy,' she muttered. ' 'Tis the way for the measles—'

'It is *not* the way,' I interrupted her. 'Stop what you are doing at once—oh, you wicked old woman, you have wakened the child with your horrible goings on.'

I ran across the room to Piram who, flushed and heavy-eyed, was crying fitfully. I cradled him in my arms and did my best to soothe him. He seemed delirious and unaware of what was taking place. My arms still about him I told the old woman once more to stop what she was doing. 'If you do not obey me,' I said in a steely voice, 'I shall go for Mr Tangye.'

She laughed. 'Fetch him,' she cried insolently, still plucking at the hapless fowl. 'He knows 'tis the way to cure the boy—'

'We shall soon see about that,' I retorted, and easing Piram gently down among the pillows again, I ran back to my room, opened the communicating door and burst in upon Nicholas. He was awake at once and stared at me in astonishment.

'Piram,' I cried. 'Come to Piram. The old nurse has gone mad—' As I spoke Nicholas was reaching for his robe. He dashed past me and headed for the child's room with the speed of a hurricane.

I followed on his heels explaining what was happening. When we reached Piram's room Nicholas took in the scene at a glance. 'Get that disgusting object out of here at once, woman,' he barked. 'Now, do you hear?' as she seemed about to defy him.

' 'Tis the cure—' she began.

'I know all about that,' Nicholas told her angrily. 'All the same, get rid of it.'

There was that in his tone which brooked of no disobedience and still muttering and arguing under her breath, she cut the fowl down and took it away.

I had gone at once to be beside Piram, and Nicholas now came over to us. The child was quieter now, but very flushed still. I stroked the dark curls back from his forehead and felt them damp beneath my hand.

Mrs Polglaze returned and Nicholas ordered her to clean up the mess. When she had done so he told her to go to the servants' quarters and make up a bed for herself. 'But I sleep in the boy's room,' she argued sullenly.

'Not any more,' she was informed curtly.

She gathered up her nightdress and other belongings from beside where she had slept at the other end of the room, and left us. Nicholas sat down on the edge of Piram's bed and gently picked up the small hand flung over the coverlet, leaning forward he rubbed it gently against his cheek. It was a gesture oddly in contrast with much of his behaviour.

I could not contain my bewilderment any longer. 'Whatever was Mrs Polglaze up to?' I asked him across the now quiet child.

'Don't tell me you have never come across such an incident before?' he said incredulously. 'You have lived in Cornwall all your life, have you not?'

'Of course,' I replied, 'but—'

'Obviously you have not come in contact with the measles before,' he interrupted wryly. 'It is an old superstition and widely believed throughout the county that what you saw the old nurse doing is a sure way of curing the disease. It is believed that within twenty-four hours the measles rash leaves the human sufferer and transfers to the still living fowl. And that when the wretched bird with a final struggle dies, the patient is found to be free from both his fever and the infection.'

'I think it is horrible,' I said shuddering.

'It is a wonder that you never heard your grandmother mention the custom,' went on Nicholas. 'I would almost take it as certain that she would have believed in it.'

'No,' I argued quickly. 'I think it highly unlikely that she would have countenanced such superstition; she was a governess in Devon, you know, before her marriage, and educated—'

'Ah!' interrupted Nicholas, 'that explains the omission in your own education regarding Cornish lore.' His eyes, as he talked with me were on the child, anxious and alert. 'I will stay with him for the rest of the night,' he announced, suddenly.

'No,' I argued. 'I will stay with him. Please, I feel it my duty.'

He rose at once, glancing down at me appraisingly. 'Then I had better fetch you your dressing-robe and some blankets to wrap around you,' he announced blandly. 'You are likely to freeze to death in your nightdress!'

I blushed furiously before the look in his eyes. Until that moment I had never given a thought to my appearance. What a brazen person he must think me, running about in the night without my robe! I did not look at him when he came back with it. My head bent, I thanked him and closed the door quickly behind him.

Piram soon slept and did not wake again throughout the night. I was glad of the blankets which Nicholas had brought me and, wrapped in them, was able to keep pleasantly warm as I sat by the nursery fire. Eventually I dozed off in my chair and did not wake until seven o'clock in the morning.

★ ★ ★ ★

During the next few days I spent almost all my time in the nursery. Piram continued to be very ill and I was consumed with anxiety. Nicholas fetched the doctor once more.

'The child is weak,' he said, 'but he has an even chance...'

When at the end of two weeks Piram took a definite turn for the better I almost wept with joy.

Mrs Polglaze, in the meantime, had been dismissed. Not dismissed from the house entirely, but from her position as nurse. Nicholas told her that as she had nowhere else to go she could live in one of the rooms above the stables and come to work in the kitchen. Mrs Bray, he told her, would find her something to do.

Every time I encountered the old woman she looked at me as though she could have killed me and it was evident that she considered her dismissal my fault. In a way I suppose I was responsible, for, totally unsatisfactory though she was, things might not have come to a head so soon, had I not discovered her at her ghastly superstitious rite.

Nicholas had decided that for the time being I was to continue to look after Piram myself. When the child was fully recovered, then, he said, he would look for another nurse. There was no one, actually, but myself to undertake the task, for I had been correct in assuming that Mrs Bray and Mrs Polglaze were the only servants in the house. But I did not in the least mind being nurse-maid. On the contrary, I was glad of the activity for it meant I had less time than I otherwise would have had in which to brood about my affairs, to make futile speculations about my parents...or my future with Nicholas...

It is strange how good sometimes results from evil things; by the time the whole harrowing experience of Piram's illness was over, the child had come to accept me completely.

'I knew that I was right,' said Nicholas exultantly when I told him that Piram had of his own accord begun to call me Mama. 'I knew that you were the sort of person he would trust.'

I smiled, inwardly delighted at the praise. 'He is still a lonely child, though,' I went on slowly, 'he ought to have someone to play with—' I stopped, aghast at the implication behind my words.

Nicholas was looking at me with ill-concealed amusement. 'You mean he should be provided with a small brother or sister?' he asked teasingly. 'Well my dear, *you* know and *I* know, that that is quite impossible; any more children that I am likely to father must of necessity be born out of wedlock, must they not?' I turned away from him, refusing to meet his eyes, and ran from the room.

In the sanctuary of the nursery I let the tears come. Piram saw them. 'Why are you crying?' he asked innocently.

'I do not know, Piram,' I told him, absolutely truthfully. 'I do not know!'

CHAPTER 8

Piram was better, completely so. Life at Trenance House was back to normal.

Not quite so fully occupied now, I found myself thinking about Lady Penelope again and about the mad woman, but especially about Lady Penelope and her veiled hint that I might be in for some dreadful trouble or other. What could the rumours she had referred to be about, I wondered. Or were there in fact, any rumours at all? Might it not be true, as Nicholas had assured me at the time, that she was trying to upset me out of spite and jealousy? Surely, I reasoned, if some danger or calamity did indeed threaten me, I would have heard hints of it from other quarters. As I had not done so, I soon had no difficulty in dismissing the insinuations completely from my mind and as the days passed smoothly and uneventfully by I began to feel more settled in my new home, less strange, not quite so apprehensive about the future; and there was also something else which contributed to this more optimistic attitude of mine.

Besides bringing Piram and me closer together, the child's illness and the consequent upheaval in the household had brought about an easing of the air of awkwardness and strain in the place generally. Nicholas seemed a little more approachable, less severe and taciturn in his manner, with fewer spates of bad temper. I began to have hopes that life with him as my husband, even though he was husband in name only, could be less empty than I had at first thought. When he was in a good humour he was charming and most excellent company, often teasing me gently in a manner I found very agreeable. As far as material things went, I lacked for nothing at all. It was clear, as he had told me in the first place, that Nicholas was exceedingly rich. Furthermore, with Mrs Bray as housekeeper I had established a most satisfactory relationship. Having taken an instant liking to her on my arrival, my regard and respect for the motherly little soul had increased daily. During Piram's illness she had worked herself well nigh to the limit; nothing had ever been too much trouble for her and she had eased my task in a thousand little thoughtful ways.

It was from her, now that life was on a more even keel once more, that I learned the reason for the lack of servants in the house; it was a strange story and in it I found the explanation to Lady Penelope's hints of impending disaster.

It had puzzled me right from the start that an establishment such as Trenance House, whose every room spoke of great wealth by the opulence and grandeur of its appointments, should be run by only two servants. I had never dared to question Nicholas about it, but one day I decided that there could be no harm in my mentioning the matter to Mrs Bray. Not being so bold as to ask her outright if she knew the reason for this strange state of affairs, I merely asked if she did not find it hard running such a house with the help only of old Mrs Polglaze.

She looked at me shrewdly a moment before answering my question. 'You be wondering about the lack of servants, mi dear, I think. Has the master not told you then?'

My heart took a strange leap. I sat down on the kitchen chair nearest to me before replying.

'No,' I told Mrs Bray, keeping my voice steady with an effort. 'The master has not mentioned the matter to me at all.'

'He must have been frightened it might upset you, I reckon,' she said thoughtfully. 'But you be a sensible young lady, not given to imaginings and the like; 't would be no harm to tell you—and somebody will even if I don't.'

My heart was beating painfully. In silence I waited for her to continue.

'It be the house, ma'am,' she said at length. 'They say it be haunted.'

I could have laughed aloud. Was that all? After the strange and formless fears that had begun to stir in me, the relief was enormous.

'Haunted?' I exclaimed. 'A ghost? Have you yourself seen it, Mrs Bray?'

She shook her head. 'No,' she told me. 'But every nursemaid we've had since the mistress died reckons as how they've seen it, and they scared the others with their tales—'

'What form does the ghost take?' I wanted to know. A guarded look crept into the little housekeeper's eyes. 'I told you, Ma'am,' she said carefully. 'I haven't seen it—'

'But what did the nursemaids say?' I pressed.

'They said it took the form of a woman, and that she knocked on the nursery window in the night.'

'And Mrs Polglaze, what about her. Is she not afraid?'

'She hasn't never heard it,' came the instant reply. 'When that one sleeps, 't would take an earthquake to waken 'er.'

'How many nursemaids have there been, Mrs Bray?'

'Three, ma'am.'

'And I suppose the whole district knows about the ghost now?'

'Yes. And even the men won't take work on the place.'

'Except your husband and son?'

'Oh, they be like me, ma'am, they wouldn't leave the master no matter what.'

'You are obviously very devoted to him, all the three of you. I'm sure he must find your loyalty to him very heart-warming.'

'We been with him a long time; he be a good master to us.'

'If there *is* a ghost,' I asked her. 'Have you any ideas about whose it could be?'

'No.' There was an air of finality in her voice that puzzled me slightly. 'And now, ma'am, if you'll excuse me, it be time I got on with the dinner.'

She got up from her rocking chair near the big, black range, and set about taking down her cooking utensils. I knew I should hear no more from her on the subject; her manner made it abundantly clear to me that as far as she was concerned, the topic was now closed, and she wanted to be left alone to get on with her work.

At first I did not connect the ghost story with Lady Penelope's talk of rumours. Then, all at once, it struck me that this was what she must have been hinting at. I smiled to myself at the thought. If the lady imagined that such stories would frighten and alarm me, then she was very much mistaken. My grandmother had had a theory about ghosts and had passed it on to me. 'If there be ghosts,' she had insisted, 'they are but souls that cannot rest; they are to be pitied not feared, for I never yet heard tell of such a creature harming anybody.'

It was a relief, even though I had managed to push them into the back of my mind, to have had the rumours finally dealt with.

My feeling of hopefulness towards the

future was increased by this circumstance and by something else: I had had no further contact or communication with the Harfords and any fears that I had harboured that they might try to hound me out of the district in spite of my marriage, proved groundless. I came to the conclusion that they either did not know of my marriage, and thought me out of their vicinity, or that they knew of it but had chosen to ignore the fact.

In making these assumptions, however, I was mistaken, as I was very soon to find out.

It happened one morning at breakfast. Looking through some papers and letters, Nicholas suddenly gave a derisive laugh.

'Just look at this,' he invited. 'It would appear that our "friends" at Fistral Castle have had news of my marriage.'

Mystified at his words I looked at the paper he had passed across to me. It was an invitation, a large, square white card, a coat of arms emblazoning the top.

'Lord and Lady Harford,' I read, *'request the pleasure of the company of Mr and Mrs Nicholas Tangye at a ball on...'* There followed the time and the date. I looked up at Nicholas.

'We shall not be going, of course?' There was a question in my voice.

'On the contrary,' came the instant rejoinder. 'On the contrary, my dear Carenza, we shall most certainly be going. I would not miss witnessing the discomfiture of his high and mighty lordship when he greets you as my wife, for anything in the world.'

'I cannot help wondering why they should have issued the invitation,' I said anxiously. 'I would have thought, from what Sir William said to me, that I was the last person in the world whom they would wish to entertain.'

Nicholas looked thoughtful. 'It may be,' he said reflectively, 'that they do not know for certain that it is you whom I have married, perhaps they have heard rumours to this effect and are anxious to find out for sure for themselves.'

'Lady Penelope knows,' I put in. 'And from her conversation in the coach on that first day I gathered that she is friendly with Lady Harford, do you not think that she will have told them—although,' I amended, 'she has been away from home—' I stopped abruptly, remembering that I had not divulged to Nicholas the fact that I had been to Lady Penelope's residence. He appeared not to notice my confusion and replied:

'Ah, yes. So she has. But she has had time enough both before she went and since she returned, to have spread the news, and Penelope, as you so rightly judged, is not one to let the grass grow under her feet, as they say.'

I made some non-committal remark and asked what I should wear for the visit to Fistral Castle; I was not, I reminded Nicholas, accustomed to paying social calls on important people.

'Any of the evening gowns we bought,' he told me, 'will be perfectly suitable, but I suggest you wear the grandest of the lot for this occasion. It might be a good idea,' he went on, 'to remind the Harfords that they are not the only people of some standing in the county.'

There was nothing I could say in reply to this. But secretly I wondered if Nicholas harboured some grudge against these people. Had be been slighted by them in some way, or made to feel inferior to them socially? It seemed that his pride had taken a blow at some time or other for him to adopt such an attitude...

'By the way,' his words broke in upon my reverie. 'How did you know that Lady Penelope had been away, Carenza? I do not recall having mentioned the fact in your presence.'

I blushed furiously before his direct question. He was looking at me searchingly and there was nothing I could do but tell the truth. 'I went to the house,' I blurted out, not looking at him, 'before Piram was ill—the day I took him on the moor—'

'But why? You didn't mention that you had been to Harris Point.'

'I had a private reason for wishing to see Lady Penelope,' I hedged. 'Although of course I didn't see her; she had already set off on her journey when I arrived.'

'And this private reason you speak of?' There was an edge now to his voice, an undertone of annoyance, that made me nervous.

'I...I would rather not reveal—' I began hesitantly, keeping my eyes downcast.

In a flash he was before me, and gripping my shoulder hard, he forced me to look up at him. Enlightenment dawned in his eyes as they met mine...

'So,' he mimicked cruelly, 'you would rather not reveal your reason? Well let me tell you, my dear Carenza, I know what it was. You wanted to hear what the rumours about me were, didn't you? You did not believe me when I assured you that Lady Penelope had spoken merely out of spite, did you?'

I was close to tears, but managed to try to defend my action.

'At the time,' I said quietly, 'I was not sure what or whom to believe. Things had happened to me with such swiftness, such overwhelming things, that I was confused, uncertain about anything or anyone, but now...' I stopped.

'Go on,' Nicholas commanded.

I chose my next words with care: 'I soon decided,' I told him slowly, 'that what you said was most probably the truth; that Lady Penelope was out to upset me. I would have had no further intention of asking her about the rumours, even if Mrs Bray had not told me about them herself.'

'Mrs Bray has told you?' There was amazement in his face, a sharpness in his voice. 'What has Mrs Bray told you?'

'About the rumours,' I replied. 'About the house being haunted.'

A look of something like relief passed

over his face. 'That is all she told you? That the house is haunted?'

I sensed a note of disquiet in his words.

'She told me about the ghost,' I said, 'about the nursemaids who were frightened by an apparition who knocked on the nursery window at dead of night.'

'And nothing more?'

'Only that the ghost takes the form of a woman and—' I stopped before the look of anger that covered his face.

'And?' he demanded.

'And that she had never herself seen the ghost,' I went on apprehensively. 'And had no idea whose ghost it could be.'

Nicholas passed a hand wearily over his forehead. As suddenly as it had appeared, his anger left him. He bent and kissed me gently on the forehead.

'Forgive me, child,' he asked humbly. 'I am, as I told you once before, a brute of fiendish temper, and unworthy of your gentleness. But believe me, I am deeply touched by your belief in me. I only pray that the day it is shattered will not come too soon.'

Before I could answer he had gone from the room. For some moments, I remained, motionless, where he had left

147

me, my thoughts in turmoil. What did he mean? What could he mean? Why should my belief in him be shattered at all?... And why was I so disturbed at the possibility that it might be... I put up my hand and touched the place on my forehead where his lips had touched me, and in a sudden revealing flash I knew the reason for my turmoil. I loved him. I loved this strange, impulsive, unpredictable man whom I had married for convenience. And I knew now why I had wept bitter tears that day in the nursery. My heart had known what my mind had refused to acknowledge, and my tears had fallen at the hopelessness of it all. For I knew that Nicholas did not return my love.

Resolutely I brushed my feelings aside. I picked up the invitation from Fistral Castle again. A Ball! I had never in my life been to a ball. Feelings of pleasurable anticipation filled me, lightening my spirits. I began to think about my beautiful new dresses, to wonder which one to wear. How right Nicholas had been to insist on my having an entirely new wardrobe of clothes. Thinking about the clothes took me back to the time we had spent in Penzance. I fell to wondering again about the men I had overheard in the night, the men to whom I had seen Nicholas talking, and as I did so a faint stirring of unease assailed me. Had I given my heart to a man who was mixed up in and had given his support to illicit doings... I who had been brought up in such a law abiding and religious household.

But even as I reasoned, I knew that I could not have done otherwise. One did not choose the man with whom one fell in love. I remembered some words that I had heard somewhere: 'Three things come unbidden: fear, jealousy and love.' I had proved the truth of them as far as love was concerned. I little knew then, how soon I was to prove the truth about fear too...

Throughout the rest of the day my mood seemed to alternate between one of depression and one of hope. I longed then, more than at any time since the death of my grandmother, for someone of my own, someone to confide in; but there was no-one to whom I could turn. I could not go to Nicholas and tell him that I loved him, that I was torn with doubts about him.

Acting on a sudden impulse I ran upstairs for my cloak and went outside. I would take a brisk walk along the cliffs. The fresh air and the sea breeze would do me good. As I passed through one of the courtyards I came across old Mrs Polglaze making towards the stables. I bade her good afternoon but she did not answer me. In the emotional state of mind that I was in I felt an urge to try to establish a better feeling between us. 'Mrs Polglaze—' I began. 'I—' I stopped before the hard, unyielding expression in her eyes. It was clear that she had become my enemy. I went on through the courtyard and left her.

After I had walked some little way along the cliff top I decided to try to find the way down to the cove. I had never been down before and as the cliffs were fairly steep I knew I should have to be very careful. The path when I found it was narrow and slippery from rain that had fallen during the night, but I managed to reach the bottom without mishap.

It was sheltered in the cove, and pleasant in spite of its being winter, and I looked about me with interest. It reminded me of the cove near my grandmother's cottage. I began to explore, glad of the diversion it afforded me. I peeped inside one or two caves, picking up the odd shell or smooth round pebble left there by the tide. Then I came upon a cave which seemed to burrow much further underneath the cliffs than the others. I peered inside it, but it was narrow, and dark, and I could not see the other end of it.

Cautiously I made my way inside for a little way, curious as to how far it might extend. I satisfied myself first that the sea was well out because I knew that all the caves could well fill up with water when the tide came in again and I had no desire to be marooned in any of them. The one I was exploring was becoming narrower, the width of a single track between rocks. The sand beneath my feet was firm, unwashed, unless I were greatly mistaken, by any tide. It was getting darker and darker as I went further inside and I began to feel nervous.

I turned sharply round to retrace my steps. It was then that I saw something white glistening in the gloom. I bent down to touch it where it lay on a flat smooth rock. It was salt; a tiny heap of salt. I did not stay to investigate further but made for the entrance of the cave with alacrity. For the presence of salt meant one thing and one thing only: smuggling. Although I had lived a very sheltered, almost cloistered life in my grandmother's cottage I had been in the company of the castle servants and of the local fisherfolk sufficiently to know of the trafficking in salt, tea, brandy and other commodities which took place. 'Fair trading' as some of the participants called their smuggling, went on all the time, I was well aware, but this was the very first time I had come upon concrete evidence of such an activity.

As I climbed back up the path which wound tortuously to the top of the cliffs my mind flew back yet again to the men I had seen with Nicholas at Penzance...it seemed as though my suspicions concerning them could be right...and then another memory surfaced in my mind; not a memory really, just something that at the time I must have noted only in my subconscious: that faint elusive smell that had hung about Nicholas's clothes the night he had found me at his gates...at the time I had been only dimly aware of something familiar, but now suddenly I realised what it was: it was the smell of the sea. Could it be that he had not come from the house that night as I had supposed, but was returning from the cove?

I wondered whether or not to mention the matter of the salt to him but decided against it. Had he not informed me that the less interest I took in his affairs the better? So be it. I had no wish to arouse his anger again.

The rest of the day I spent with Piram. The child and I were now firm friends and every day he seemed to grow in confidence and self-assurance. Playing games with him and listening to his childish prattle I was able for a while to forget the things that were troubling me. More than that, I clung to the hope that my deep love for the child must somehow eventually forge a bond between myself and his father. It was a thought that gave me comfort.

CHAPTER 9

As the day of the ball at Fistral Castle drew nearer, I began to have many misgivings about attending it. For one thing, I felt sure that Penelope would be among the guests and I had no stomach for another encounter with her.

The fact was that I was just no match for her; her particular brand of spitefulness, her sly innuendos, were weapons against which I had no defence. On top of this I was frightened, since she was a great friend of Lady Marion, that she would have been told about my visit to the castle and about the locket and the letter: if the Harford's had hinted to her that I was a bastard, she would not fail to use such information to my discomfiture, of that I was certain. And I did not relish seeing the Harfords themselves again. I mistrusted them and their motive in inviting me.

All this I blurted out to Nicholas in an attempt to have him refuse the invitation, but he was adamant about our going.

'What about Piram?' I asked in desperation. 'Mrs Bray has too many duties to attend to without having the added burden of attending to a child in the evening.'

'Arrangements have been made to take care of that,' I was told promptly. 'Mrs Bray has asked a niece of hers, from Newquay, to come and look after Piram.'

'And has she agreed—in spite of the rumours?' I could have bitten off my tongue, but the words were out before I could stop them.

A dark look flashed in Nicholas's sea blue eyes, but he made no reference to my outburst.

'I have just told you,' he said coldly. 'It is all arranged. The girl's name, by the way, is Jenny and if she seems suitable, I shall take her on as nursemaid on a permanent basis.'

There was no way out for me it seemed. I should have to visit Fistral Castle whether I wanted to or not.

And so the day of the ball arrived. All day long I was in a state of nervousness about it. Yet, strangely, it was a nervousness that was tinged with excitement. I felt a surge of gratitude towards my dear grandmother for having bothered, old as she had been, to teach me the art of dancing. I had been an apt pupil, she had told me, and it was comforting to know that at least in this respect I should be able to acquit myself reasonably well.

Nicholas had decided which dress I was to wear. It was made of rich, cream silk and had a wide fichu neckline, embroidered with hundreds of small pearls. I was glad as I surveyed myself in the mirror that my shoulders were rounded and smooth for the dress revealed them to the full. The sheen of the silk seemed to bring a glow to my pale skin and I was not displeased at my reflection.

For this special event I had altered my hair and had scooped up my long black ringlets and wound them round my head. It had the effect, I thought, of making me look a little older than I usually looked, but this pleased me and gave me more self-confidence.

Nicholas was waiting for me in the hall. He turned as I came towards him, a surprised expression on his face. He looked so devastatingly handsome in his evening clothes that I could have died with love for him and I had difficulty in preventing myself from revealing it in my eyes.

'You look quite beautiful,' he said the words lightly as he took my arm and led me outside to the waiting carriage. 'I shall be proud of you.'

I inclined my head at the compliment, pleased, yet disappointed, for his words though sincere and kind, had no warmth about them.

Nicholas wrapped the rugs around me, and called to the coachman to set off.

We did not talk much during the journey. Ever since I had realised that I was in love with Nicholas, I had become increasingly tongue-tied with him. Forever on my guard not to reveal my innermost feelings, my conversation was largely stilted and unnatural. Nicholas, for his part, seemed lately to be both moody and withdrawn.

Just before we reached the castle he smiled across at me and my heart lurched sickeningly.

'Don't be so nervous,' he said kindly. 'Try to see the funny side of the situation; be a bit more like me and anticipate with pleasure the discomfiture of the Harfords when they see you.'

'I wish with all my heart that I could,' I told him earnestly. 'But it is not my nature to be so, I'm afraid; and I cannot help but feel a little fearful, remembering my last visit to this place—'

'Look,' interrupted Nicholas, drawing aside the window curtains. 'Look, we are nearly there. You can see the castle now.'

I followed his gaze. 'How beautiful it looks in the moonlight,' I murmured, strangely moved by the awesome grandeur before me. Tears stung my eyes suddenly and Nicholas looked at me in concern.

'Are you all right, Carenza?' he asked sharply. I nodded, incapable of speech.

Desperately I fought to control myself; to calm the tumult within me.

'Why, you're shaking all over,' there was alarm now in Nicholas's voice; 'What is it, Carenza, what is the matter?'

'I don't know,' I whispered hoarsely. 'The castle...it's so beautiful and yet—'

'Yet what?' he interrupted.

'Yet it fills me with fear,' I replied slowly. 'I feel as though I love it and hate it both at the same time; do you understand?'

'No,' he replied impatiently. 'I do not. You are talking utter nonsense—fanciful Cornish nonsense—the effects of the sea and the moonlight on your sensitive soul.'

The carriage came to a standstill in the castle courtyard. 'Come,' Nicholas took my hand and helped me to the ground. 'We are here. Away with your silly fears; this is a night to enjoy.' He smiled at me reassuringly, tucked my arm in his and led me to the castle entrance.

'Mr and Mrs Nicholas Tangye.' The flunkey's voice intoned the words and I found myself once more looking into the face of Sir William Harford. For a fleeting second a look of startled incredulity passed over his features, replaced almost immediately by one of bland, polite informality.

Nicholas, deliberately provocative, made the introductions. 'I believe, Harford, that you have already had the pleasure of meeting my wife?'

A dull flush suffused the podgy face before me. 'A mistake,' he muttered uncomfortably, turning to his wife for support. 'We made a mistake, didn't we, Marion?...'

His wife nodded, her plain face full of embarrassment, 'We had no idea...' her words tailed off. 'I mean, it was all so sudden and...' She stopped, looking self-consciously towards her husband.

I decided to come to their rescue. 'Please do not let the matter trouble you,' I said calmly. 'I assure you it is of no consequence to me at all.'

We walked past them, making our way towards the dancing. Nicholas pulled me behind a pillar; he was shaking with suppressed laughter. 'Superb,' he almost choked. 'You were utterly superb. I shall *never* forget that little episode to my dying day.' And almost swinging me off my feet he took me in his arms and started dancing with me gaily.

We seemed to be the centre of all eyes and I was glad that Nicholas had told me I looked beautiful and that he would be proud of me; it served to make me less self-conscious than I otherwise would have been. Dancing with him was sweet torment, for as he held me, desire and longings such as I had never imagined inflamed my whole being, and I had to exercise every ounce of willpower that I possessed, not to press myself close to him and fling my arms about his neck.

As courtesy demanded he danced with Lady Marion once but from the look on his face I did not think he enjoyed the experience; others may not have noticed, but knowing him as I did, I was able to recognise the signs of boredom that his good manners were only just able to conceal. He came over to me when the dance was over and asked how I was enjoying myself.

'Very much,' I smiled up at him. 'I have danced with Sir William, by the way, and he has suggested that we make another visit to the castle tomorrow when he and Lady Marion are alone.'

'Oh, indeed!' Nicholas sounded surprised. 'Did he give any reason in particular for wanting the pleasure of our company again so soon?'

'Yes.' I nodded. 'He considers that he owes me an absolute apology, it seems and—'

'So he does,' interrupted Nicholas.

'And,' I continued. 'He says that there is something more concerning me that he would like to discuss with us both; and as it is of a strictly private nature he didn't consider that tonight was an expedient time to do so.'

'True enough,' agreed Nicholas. 'Did he, by any chance say whether he knew that it was you I had married, before he saw you tonight?'

'He said he had heard that you had married a young girl by the name of Pearce, a young lady unknown in this area, and having remembered my name from my calling here, had wondered...'

'But he hadn't been sure, eh?' cut in Nicholas. 'And by the look on his face when he saw you, I fancy he had hoped that you were *not* the lady concerned.'

'I wish that you had not insisted on my coming,' I replied unhappily. 'I feel that I am an embarrassment to them.'

'Nonsense,' Nicholas said roundly. 'They invited you, did they not? It follows that they wanted you here for some reason.'

'Perhaps,' I admitted. 'But it seems more likely to me that they wanted *you* here, and could not invite you without me now that I am your...your wife.'

Nicholas gave me a searching look as I hesitated over the word wife.

'Why do you—' he began. But at that point Lady Penelope came up to us and put an end to our conversation. My dislike of her at once increased for I would dearly have loved to hear what Nicholas was about to ask me.

'Where have you two love-birds been hiding?' she asked archly. 'I have been looking for you for ages.' She smiled provocatively at Nicholas as she spoke and put an almost proprietary hand on his arm. 'I'm quite sure you are going to ask me to dance, Nicholas, and it just so happens that the next one is free.' She gave me a dazzling smile. 'Dear Carenza will not mind lending you to me, will you my child?'

I replied that my husband was at liberty to dance with whom he chose, of course. He looked at me through narrowed eyes for a second and then without a word led Lady Penelope to the floor.

I could not suppress the sudden pang of jealousy that smote me at the sight of them together. She was so beautiful, the most outstanding woman in the room, with her superbly cut gown of crimson silk and her magnificent diamonds. Tall, almost in fact as tall as Nicholas, she made a perfect dancing partner for him and I saw many heads turn in their direction as they circled the ballroom. Nicholas did not look bored this time. And yet, I reflected, struggling to quell my jealousy, he spoke of her in disparaging terms, intimated that she pursued him and that he had no time for her; and it was I whom he had married...

A lump in my throat, I turned my back on the brilliant scene in front of me and went to sit in a quiet secluded alcove beneath the minstrel's gallery. I was behind some palms and flowers and out of sight. Suddenly I heard a man talking somewhere quite close to me but I could see nobody. 'That wife of Tangye's,' I heard him say.

'Whom does she remind you of?'

'Damned if I know,' came an answering voice. 'It's been badgering me ever since I clapped eyes on her.' The two moved off out of earshot and I heard no more.

It was then that I noticed Lady Marion; she must have come up behind me and been standing fairly near but I had not heard her. It was the sudden sharp intake of breath that made me turn and see her; her face was as white as china clay. Whether she had seen me or not I did not know, nor whether she had heard the two men, but something or somebody had certainly upset her. She moved swiftly away from the alcove and set off down the side of the ballroom weaving her way along the colonnade of pillars, her eyes darting this way and that as if she were looking for someone.

Fascinated, I watched her. It was quickly apparent that it was her husband whom she was seeking. He was standing alone, helping himself to a glass of wine from a tray held by a servant. Waving the footman aside, Lady Marion almost threw herself upon Sir William. Naturally I could not hear what she was saying, but there was no mistaking the urgency of her manner. Her husband listened intently, his gaze never leaving her face. They seemed, I thought, to be deliberating about something, their heads close together, their faces worried.

Suddenly, Lady Marion beckoned a hovering footman. She said something to him and the servant put down his tray of wine glasses and followed her out of the ballroom. I could see which door they went through and I was still looking at it, wondering where it led to, when it opened again and Lady Marion came back into the ballroom. Her face was calmer now and she walked over to talk with some of her guests in a composed manner. Obviously whatever had upset her was now settled and she resumed her position as gracious hostess once more.

I thought it was time I rejoined Nicholas and turned to go and look for him, but a sudden wave of sickness came over me and I decided that I needed some fresh air. I was near the door which Lady Marion had come through and so I slipped through it. I found myself in a narrow passage, dimly lit, and at the end of it I could see a flight of stairs. I made my way up them thinking they might lead to some balcony or other where I could be in the open.

Once at the top I discovered that I was on a narrow landing and I was just in time to see the retreating figure of the footman at the far end. He turned a corner out of my sight and I hurried after him, intending to ask him to direct me. The narrow landing led to a much wider, deeply carpeted one that was well lit.

My feet made no sound as I walked along and the footman was obviously unaware of my presence. He stopped in front of a door with two steps leading up to it. I did not like to follow him and decided I should have to try to find my own way. When I drew just about level with the door it re-opened and he came out again. To my amazement I saw that he was carrying a picture. He did not seem in the least surprised at my presence on the landing.

'I reckon you'm lost, missie,' he said kindly, before I could explain. 'I'll put the picture in the cupboard and then show you the way back to the ballroom.' He was holding the picture so that its back was towards me but when he put it down to open the cupboard doors a little further along the landing, he turned it round.

Mildly interested I glanced at it. I saw that it was a portrait of a young man.

He was very handsome and there was something vaguely familiar about his face but I could not determine what it was.

'I do not wish to return to the ballroom just yet,' I explained. 'I came up here in the hopes of finding my way to some balcony or other where I could get a breath of fresh air; perhaps you will be good enough to direct me.'

'Best go through the picture gallery,' he replied at once, ' 'tis the quickest way; follow me, missie.' He led the way back along the wide landing and re-opened the door he had just come out from. As I followed him I saw that we were in a long picture gallery, a gallery whose walls were almost completely covered with pictures. Most of them, or at least most of those that I caught a glimpse of as we passed quickly through, were portraits.

About half way along the length of the wall on my right, I noticed a gap and idly concluded that the picture the footman had put in the landing cupboard had formerly hung there. The place was only moderately well lighted and I could not see any of the pictures very clearly nor discern any names above or below them.

We were leaving the gallery now and

making our way down a passage at right angles to it. A few yards along, it widened into a sizeable square with two further corridors, one to the right and one to the left leading from it. The footman took the left passage and stopped in front of the first door that we came to.

'There is a balcony leading from this room, miss,' he informed me, opening the door. 'The room is not in use and it will be perfectly in order for you to pass through it.' He left the door open so that I could see my way across the unlit room by the glow which came from the lamps in the corridor. As I stepped into that room, the strangest sensation came over me. I felt at once that I knew it, that I had been there before; and the feeling I had experienced on seeing the castle in the moonlight returned to me. As then, a disturbing undertone of fear fought for dominance over the feeling of belonging...

I left the room abruptly. 'I've changed my mind,' I told the footman. 'Please show me the way back to the ballroom right away.'

He was an old man and he looked at me shrewdly before setting off down the corridor. 'You'm sure you be all right, missie?' he asked courteously. 'You'm pale looking.'

I assured him that I was perfectly well and told him to lead the way.

As we walked along I made a great effort to calm myself down again. Mentally I shook myself. What on earth was the matter with me? Such absurdity to imagine I knew the room. I had never been near it or anywhere like it in my life before. Perhaps it was the effect of the wine I had drunk. After all I was not yet accustomed to drinking it. I decided that I would not mention the incident to Nicholas. Doubtless if I did he would put it down to my 'sensitive Cornish soul' again and laugh at me.

As I remembered his phrase, a startling thought hit me: Nicholas invariably referred to me as being Cornish, but in view of my mother's German name I could at most only be half so...perhaps not even that. I wished with all my heart that I knew.

For one bitter moment I wished that my grandmother had kept her secret; that she had never revealed to me that I was anything other than her granddaughter as I had always supposed myself to be. At least I should have felt I had a right to my name, even though it be a humble one.

But my bitterness was short lived when I remembered that had this been the case I would never have met Nicholas...

We had reached the top of the flight of stairs down to the first passage.

'I can find my own way now, thank you,' I said to the footman. I walked past him and down the stairs. At the bottom I turned and looked round. He was still standing where I had left him, a baffled expression on his face. When he realised that I was looking at him, he muttered something which I did not catch and shuffled away down a narrow corridor to his left.

Slowly I approached the door which would take me back to the ballroom, willing myself to dismiss from my thoughts all my fanciful ideas. A determined smile on my face, I opened the door. At once the blazing lights, the glittering scene, the gaiety and music brought me back to normality. I was myself again.

Back in the ballroom I made my way towards Nicholas whom I could see talking with a group of men.

'I missed you,' he greeted me. 'Where have you been?'

I felt abruptly pleased. I had been away from the room barely ten minutes. 'It was a little overpowering,' I explained. 'The noise, the warmth, the scent of the flowers. I went for a breath of air.'

There seemed to be a general move towards the supper-room just then and we made our way along. It was the most sumptuous array of food I had ever seen in my life, surpassing even the banquets I had seen being prepared at Tregonning Castle. There was such a vast number of dishes that I should have been completely at a loss which to choose had not Nicholas decided for me. For most of the time we were surrounded by people laughing and talking and there was little opportunity for private conversation. But just before we were to return to the ballroom I got a chance to tell Nicholas about the picture.

He frowned. 'An odd time of night to be moving pictures around, I would have thought,' he said slowly. 'Yes,' I agreed. 'It is—unless—' I stopped as a sudden thought struck me.

'Unless what?' Nicholas questioned.

'Well something else happened earlier,'

I explained and went on to tell him about the conversation I had overheard and about the look of alarm on Lady Marion's face. 'It has just occurred to me that there *could* be a connection...at the time I did not associate the one with the other...'

Nicholas was looking thoughtful. 'Could you find the cupboard again?' he asked suddenly.

'Certainly.'

'Then take me to it,' he commanded. 'I have a mind to take a look at this picture myself; something tells me there is more to this than meets the eye.'

But when we reached the cupboard and opened the doors we found that it was empty. The picture had gone.

'Wrong cupboard,' said Nicholas at once.

'No,' I was emphatic. 'I am absolutely sure that this is the one.' I tried to make light of it. 'What a fuss we're making about nothing; the footman has no doubt taken the picture somewhere downstairs to clean the frame or something.'

'I expect so,' Nicholas replied, but both from the tone of his voice and from the puzzled look on his face, I knew that he did not accept my explanation; and

I wasn't sure that I believed it myself. I had an uneasy feeling about it.

Lady Penelope cornered me before we left the ball. I was standing on my own waiting for Nicholas who was arranging with Sir William the time of our visit to Fistral Castle on the morrow.

'I have been wanting an opportunity to speak to you alone my dear, all evening,' she gushed. 'You look quite radiant and happy, but then I have no doubt that you are well versed in the art of concealing your real feelings.' Her voice had changed to one of commiseration. 'Tell me how things really are,' she urged.

Her attitude annoyed me. I did not need pity from anybody, least of all her.

'I'm afraid I do not understand you, Lady Penelope,' I said stiffly, and made as if to turn away from her.

Immediately her manner changed. An ugly look came over her face. 'Pray do not imagine that you can play the lady with me,' she hissed. 'I know about you.'

I felt the colour flooding my face. So, Lady Marion *had* told her, just as I thought she would. Making a desperate attempt at some semblance of dignity I said: 'In that case Lady Penelope, I feel sure you would rather not converse with me at all.'

Again I tried to walk away from her but even as I moved, her hand shot out and grabbed my arm; I was surprised at the strength of her grip.

'Oh no you don't.' There was a viciousness about her tone that alarmed me and I did not struggle against her. 'You will remain here until I have had my say.'

She leaned closer to me. 'Go back where you belong,' she whispered harshly. 'Back to your own sort of people—common people. Nicholas is a fool to himself. He acts without thinking. You are no good to him. When the news about you gets round, as it will, he will be ruined socially.'

Tears threatened to overwhelm me in the face of her cruel words. For the life of me I could not utter one word in my own defence. Seizing her advantage over me, she went on:

'This is the second mistake Nicholas has made; he will live to regret this one just as he did the first—'

'What do you mean?' I managed to cry out.

'Nothing,' she replied promptly, a secretive look in her eyes. 'But if you know what is good for you, *Miss* Pearce, you will leave

Trenance House just as fast as you can.'
And with that she swept away and left me.

I realised then that I was trembling from head to foot. I looked anxiously around for Nicholas and saw that he was busy talking still. Fighting back my tears I groped my way to a quiet corner of the great hall at the opposite end from which the guests were assembling ready for their departure. I sank wearily onto a wooden settle in an alcove, which was more or less screened from view, hoping no one would notice me. I intended to remain there only for a minute or two until I had composed myself. I had hardly sat down when I realised with a start that there was already someone there; the place had no light of its own, and was only faintly illuminated by the candles in the hall but even in the gloom I could see who it was who crouched there; it was the mad woman. Once or twice during the evening I had thought of her and wondered whether I would see her.

She did not seem surprised to see me. 'I'm glad you've come again,' she said agreeably.

I smiled wearily but made no reply.

'I sit here and watch sometimes,' she

went on, 'instead of in the gallery; I can hear more.' Suddenly she thrust her face close to mine. 'What are you crying for?' she demanded.

I replied that I wasn't really crying, just that my eyes were tired and watery.'

'That's good,' she replied. 'I don't want you to be sad; I like you, you see.' She patted my hand in a friendly gesture.

'Thank you.' I smiled at her. She was peering now round the end of the alcove.

'I don't like *her*,' she announced suddenly, pointing a long thin finger towards the opposite end of the hall. I followed her gaze and saw that it was Lady Penelope to whom she was referring.

'Bad,' she muttered, almost to herself. 'Bad.' A secretive, sly look stole into the staring eyes. 'I saw her on the cliffs, I did; at home all night, was she?'

She seemed to be working herself up into a fury about something so I deemed it wise to make my getaway. I do not think she even noticed my going.

Nicholas was in the hall and obviously looking around for me. I was more than ready to join him; to be in the company of someone agreeable and reassuringly normal.

'You are exceptionally quiet.' It was Nicholas speaking on our way home.

'I am very tired,' I replied evasively.

He looked at me searchingly. 'I saw you talking with Penelope. Have you been so silly as to let her upset you again?'

Stung by his tone I promptly denied such a thing. 'Certainly not,' I replied indignantly.

'Well I'm glad to hear it,' he told me. 'Glad that you have learned to take no notice of her. She takes a delight in upsetting people.'

I did not reply. This was a subject I would rather not talk about. We both lapsed into silence.

Just as the carriage drew into the courtyard of Trenance House Nicholas spoke again. 'She is certainly a very beautiful woman, whatever else,' he said thoughtfully. The words were like a knife thrust in my heart. Had he been thinking about her then all the time we had been silent; it seemed so. I bid him goodnight and went to my bed with a heavy heart.

It was a long time before I slept. I kept going over the evening's events in my mind. About the room with the balcony, the picture, and above all, Lady Penelope and the mad woman.

Suddenly I became aware of footsteps and sat up in bed with a start. I listened carefully, my heart thumping and then I relaxed back among the pillows as I realised that the sounds came from the adjoining room. It was clear that Nicholas was pacing up and down, his footsteps purposely quiet, I guessed, so as not to disturb me. It appeared that he too was unable to sleep.

Miserably I wondered what it could be that bothered him enough to keep him awake. Could it be that, as Lady Penelope had hinted, he was already beginning to regret his hasty marriage? The rest of the happenings at the castle paled into insignificance beside such a bitter thought.

CHAPTER 10

I got up next morning in what I considered to be a more sensible frame of mind. Away with turbulent emotions I told myself, and concentrate on practical matters. The marriage between Nicholas and myself had done all that was required of it: I had a home, a name and security, Nicholas had a mother for his son. It was stupid to give way to thoughts of what might have been and there was neither virtue nor reward in doing so. With a deliberately brisk and purposeful air I joined Nicholas for breakfast.

'You did say that we were to visit Fistral Castle after lunch, did you not?' I asked him as I sat down opposite him. He nodded absently, intent on a letter he held in his hand. 'Oh, I do beg your pardon,' I apologised at once. 'I did not realise you were occupied with something.'

He did not seem to hear me and I noticed that his face wore a very pre-occupied expression. I wondered what it could be that was causing him to look so troubled. He had told me nothing of his business affairs apart from the fact that he owned several farms and a mine. As far as I could determine, the paper he was studying so carefully seemed to be a list of something. Perhaps it was a report from the mine, I thought, a list of quantities or sums of money. I knew little of such matters and found anything to do with figures tedious. My mind flew back to the days of my childhood and the lessons my grandmother had given me.

Words, those were what I had loved, right from the beginning; books had always given me enormous pleasure and it seemed that there never had been a time when I couldn't read. There must have been of course, but I didn't remember it.

Nicholas was folding the papers, 'Did you say something, Carenza?'

I repeated my question and was told that we were to leave for Fistral Castle at one-thirty. 'You had better order lunch for twelve-thirty,' he suggested, 'and we will start out immediately afterwards.'

'Do you wish Piram to accompany us?' I asked.

He considered a moment or two and then said: 'No. Let him stay and play. Adult conversation can be excruciatingly boring for a small child.'

I smiled. 'I agree absolutely,' I told him. 'I am going along to the nursery now, have you time to join us for a few minutes?' I asked the question in as casual a voice as I could muster, inwardly longing for him to reply in the affirmative. The times we spent together with Piram were now very precious to me for they seemed somehow to bring Nicholas close to me for a little while.

He shook his head, rising from his chair as he did so. 'I'm afraid not; not this morning. There are matters at the mine which demand my immediate attention.'

I hid my disappointment with what I hoped was a look of understanding, and went up to the nursery alone.

Jenny our temporary nurse, greeted me tearfully. She had, it appeared, during our night at the ball, had trouble with Mrs Polglaze. The old woman had barged into the nursery and been very abusive. I consoled the distressed girl as best I could, inwardly hoping that the episode had not made her anxious to leave the place. I decided that it could do no harm to tell the girl that Nicholas intended asking her to stay on.

'I don't know whether Mr Tangye has mentioned it yet, Jenny,' I told her, 'but we would both like you to stay as Piram's nurse on a permanent footing.' She flushed with pleasure.

'Thank you, Ma'am,' she sniffed. 'I'll be pleased to, just so long as that old witch leaves me alone.'

'Leave it to me,' I assured her. 'I'll take

steps at once to see that she doesn't trouble you again.'

It was time for Piram's walk and I decided that Jenny might just as well begin taking him right away.

'Go as far as the deer park unless he tires too soon,' I suggested. 'He loves to go there, and even if you're not fortunate enough to catch a glimpse of a deer, Piram enjoys seeing the stream and the groves of trees.'

'Where is it, ma'am?'

'Oh, less than a mile from the house, Jenny; it is surrounded by a sort of palisade.' I walked over to the window and pointed out the direction in which it lay.

After I had seen the two of them off, I went in search of Mrs Polglaze. The sooner she realised that her outrageous behaviour would not be tolerated, the better. I found her in the kitchen helping Mrs Bray, and asked her to follow me to the morning room.

What I had to say did not take long. She was not to visit the nursery again. Mr Tangye had dismissed her from her post as nurse. Piram was no longer her concern. I was as pleasant as I could be and finished off by saying that I hoped I had made myself clear.

'Yes,' she stated flatly, hatred in her eyes.

I told her she could go. As she went through the door she muttered something under her breath; I only caught one word and that was not distinctly, but it sounded for all the world like 'foreigner'. I looked at the old woman sharply but she was shuffling off down the hall back to the kitchens. There was something slightly frightening about her and involuntarily I shuddered. What had she meant by 'foreigner'? She knew nothing about me, could never have seen my grandmother's letter, the letter telling of my mother's foreign-sounding name... I shrugged my shoulders and decided that she probably considered anyone not born in her immediate vicinity a foreigner; to give the matter so much as a second thought was ridiculous.

As arranged, we set off for Fistral Castle at two o'clock. I asked how Nicholas had found things at the mine and received a non-committal answer.

'About as I expected,' he replied evasively. I looked at him questioningly, expecting him to elaborate but all he said was: 'I don't propose to go into details about it; I'm quite sure you would find the subject a bore.'

I looked at him thoughtfully, and noting the worried expression he wore, wondered if all were not well at the mine. But I knew better than to persist with my questioning, having learned from experience that it was something he would not tolerate.

'I may be going away for a while very shortly,' he announced, almost casually, just before we reached our destination. His words took me completely by surprise.

'Oh,' I jerked out, my heart dropping, 'where—' I stopped. It was no business of mine where he went and he was under no obligation whatsoever to confide in me. 'I mean,' I went on lamely, 'is it on business?'

'In a sense, yes,' came the answer. We were entering the inner courtyard of the castle. The horses came to a standstill. There was no time to say more.

The Harfords greeted us effusively. How different, I mused, is my reception today from that of my original visit. We were taken into a sumptuously appointed drawing-room which opened off the great hall. Tapestries which I guessed were almost priceless, adorned the walls and the oriental carpet was the thickest and most luxurious I had ever seen in my life. The windows looked out over the sea, giving a magnificent vista of the rolling, swelling Atlantic surf. Huge log fires burned at each end of the room. We were invited to sit on a deep crimson sofa liberally supplied with the softest velvet cushions.

The Harfords, I thought, seemed nervous, ill at ease. I wondered if Nicholas noticed it. When we were all four seated in front of the fire, Sir William glanced furtively at his wife, cleared his throat and began to speak.

'You are no doubt wondering about the purpose of your visit here—'

'We are indeed,' interrupted Nicholas with his typical forthrightness of approach.

'Yes, well,' Sir William coughed nervously, his eyes darting from one to the other of us, 'the truth of the matter is, Tangye, that Marion and I have had second thoughts about your wife's claim—'

'My wife's claim?' Nicholas, a puzzled note in his voice, was, I knew, being deliberately obtuse. 'What claim, Sir William?'

The poor man looked uncomfortably towards me. 'I thought...' he began, 'that is, I presumed that you had told your husband of the letter...'

I decided to come to his aid. 'I did, Sir William,' I intervened. 'And about the locket, too; it was the word "claim" I expect which confused my husband. As far as I am aware, the letter from my grandmother made no actual claim on my behalf.' With a half-reproachful look on my face I smiled across at Nicholas; the amused glint in his eyes told me that I was right in my assessment of his behaviour and that he approved my reaction to it. A sudden glow at this affinity between us warmed my heart.

Sir William was speaking again. 'I meant no offence by using the word,' he apologised hastily. 'The fact of the matter is that my wife and I feel now that we were too hasty...isn't that so, Marion?'

His wife nodded, her plain face wearing a fulsome smile.

'To continue,' went on her husband. 'We have had a further look at the locket, have scrutinized it in effect, and we have come to the conclusion that we made a mistake.'

I half-rose from the sofa, excitement suddenly churning inside me. With a deft, firm hand, Nicholas prevented my getting to my feet. He gave me a swift, meaningful glance, then turning to our host asked quietly, 'What kind of a mistake, Sir William?'

His wife took up the story. 'There was a cousin of William's,' she said carefully. 'He spent a lot of time abroad and neither of us was close to him—'

'Whose cousin was he?' Nicholas cut in. 'Yours, Lady Marion, or your husband's?'

The question seemed to surprise her. 'Oh, William's of course,' she replied at once. 'His name was Hanson, Rupert Hanson.'

My heartbeats quickened at her words. 'And the picture in the locket, Lady Harford,' I asked eagerly. 'You think it is he?'

'Indeed we do,' she affirmed. 'Both of us. At the time of your visit we did not give him a thought...but afterwards we fell to wondering...'

'And where is he now, may I ask?' It was Nicholas speaking.

'Oh he died many years ago,' Sir William took up the story. 'That was why we didn't immediately bring him to mind. He died on the South Coast somewhere, only having recently returned from the Continent—or so we heard.'

There was one question I was aching to ask. Whatever the answer turned out to be, I knew I must ask it. Taking all my courage in both hands I asked: 'Do you know if he was married?'

A swift, unfathomable glance passed between the Harfords before Sir William replied carefully: 'We believe that he was. We did hear many years after his death that he had married a German girl—'

'The name on the locket,' I broke in, tears of thankfulness in my eyes. 'That surely is a German name—'

'Exactly,' agreed Lady Marion. 'It *is* a German name and as the locket was worn by your mother, it would seem that...'

'That the two of them were my parents,' I finished for her. Tears were spilling down my face now and unashamedly I let them fall. At last the mystery was solved. I knew who I was! I was a Harford; a member of this great family! And I had not been born out of wedlock after all. I could hold up my head along with anybody.

A sobering thought pulled me up. 'I

wonder,' I said slowly, 'why she wore no wedding ring? And how she came to die alone in such dreadful circumstances?'

Again the swift glance between the two. 'Your mother?' It was Lady Marion speaking. 'She probably had to sell the ring to obtain food; from what we have gathered, Rupert died before you were born and as she was a foreigner presumably she had no family of her own in England to turn to.'

'But she had the Harfords.' There was an edge to Nicholas's voice belying the polite smile on his face.

'She did not turn to us,' Sir William defended himself with alacrity.

'But you could have approached her, could you not?' Nicholas made the suggestion with the utmost politeness.

'You forget,' Sir William was clearly annoyed. 'We did not know of our cousin's death until many years after it had taken place; we were not in close touch with that branch of the family at any time.'

'All the same it seems strange that you did not hear of his death sooner,' Nicholas argued.

'I agree,' put in Lady Marion. 'On the face of it, Mr Tangye, it does, but there is the possibility that he was lost at sea, in some gale or other. It appears that he made frequent journeys to the Continent, as we have already told you...we did not hear how he had died remember, only that he had done so.' Lady Harford's words had brought a picture into my mind: the picture of my mother lying on the rocks. Could it be that she had been cast there from the same shipwreck that had cost her husband his life? Could not her wedding ring have been washed from her hand by the sea?

'We shall obviously never know exactly what happened to our cousin, or when.' Sir William's words broke in one my reverie. 'What is past is finished and done with.' He turned towards me: 'We cannot help either him or your poor mother, now; sufficient be it to say that we welcome you, whom we believe to be their child, as a relative.'

He was smiling now in the same fulsome way as his wife. I wished that I could have felt some liking for them. But I couldn't. They might be sincere in their welcome, and genuinely sorry for the mistake they had made, but though I was joyous at the thought of belonging to the Harford family, I could summon up no feelings of affection whatsoever for these two members of it. Forcing myself to smile agreeably I thanked him for his kindness. Lady Harford was repeating effusively the gist of what her husband had said. Taking my hand in her own small plump one, she gushed: 'And we want you to know that you are most welcome here at any time you please, dear Carenza; make the castle your second home and whenever your husband is absent from Trenance House for any period of time, you must not hesitate to come and stay with us.'

I chided myself inwardly for not feeling able to respond to her overtures with warmth and enthusiasm. 'It is most generous of you, Lady Marion,' I replied. 'But I do not like to leave Piram any more often than is absolutely necessary.'

'Ah, yes.' Lady Marion looked across at Nicholas. 'Your poor motherless little boy...' Some formless innuendo in her tone puzzled me. I glanced quickly across at Nicholas and saw the flash of anger, instantly veiled, which filled his eyes.

'Piram is no longer a poor, motherless boy, Lady Harford,' he corrected urbanely. 'On the contrary, he has the most loving mother a child could wish for.' I flashed a grateful smile in his direction, absurdly happy at the unexpected tribute. Lady Marion flashed a brilliant smile, 'Splendid, how very convenient,' she said smoothly. 'It must have taken quite a weight of responsibility off your shoulders.' The words were spoken pleasantly enough but again I felt that there was a slightly offensive nuance about her tone; and there was something about the way the two of them were eyeing each other, a wariness, that set me wondering...Lady Marion turned back to me. 'Anyway, my dear,' she remarked, 'Remember what I have said. We are your friends. If ever you need help from us at any time, you have only to ask.'

'That such a situation should arise is highly unlikely, I think,' I replied, a little annoyed. 'All my needs are more than adequately met at Trenance House, as you surely must know.' I looked nervously across at Nicholas as I spoke, but he seemed not to have heard this last exchange between Lady Marion and myself and was giving all his attention to Sir William. It was certainly a relief to me, for I had the suspicion that had he heard what had been said to me he might have been very angry indeed and lost his temper.

Over tea conversation drifted to general matters such as the weather, the state of the roads, servants. I told them about the trouble we had had with old Mrs Polglaze and they seemed most sympathetic.

'I hear you have been having difficulty in obtaining servants.' It was Lady Marion speaking and although she was smiling pleasantly as she made the observation I did not fail to detect the hint of triumph and malice behind it. I wondered what sort of reply Nicholas would give her. As I had expected, he was more than a match for her. With a smile to equal hers he replied smoothly: 'It is possible that you have heard such a thing, I am sure, but may I remind you that it is never wise to believe all that one hears Lady Harford.'

Sir William interposed with some remark about estate management at this point and so the subject of servants was abandoned. It was obvious to me that he too, sensed the veiled animosity between his wife and Nicholas and was anxious to prevent further and perhaps more malicious exchanges between them.

I fell to wondering what it could have

been that had brought about such a situation; it struck me suddenly that Lady Marion could not be very far away from Nicholas in age, a year or two older perhaps but no more. Could there have been a broken romance, or a case of unrequited love here? It seemed possible...

'Would you like to look round the castle?' Lady Marion's words brought me back to reality. I pulled myself together.

'Very much,' I answered with alacrity, then glancing across at Nicholas, 'that is if you are agreeable and if we have time?'

Nicholas nodded and rose from the couch.

We followed the Harfords from the room and began our tour of the castle. It was a vast place and contained many valuable treasures in the way of porcelain, tapestries, furniture and silver. As we went from room to room, Sir William became eloquent on the respective valuables each one contained. He also told us a great deal of the history of the place and it was clear to see that he loved every stick and stone of his magnificent home and was almost fanatically proud of his family's history. I would not like, I mused, to be in the shoes of anyone who tried to besmirch the Harford name or honour... 'Five hundred years,' he was saying proudly, 'and never a breath of scandal has touched our name; the name Harford is respected throughout the country.'

We were making our way up the steps to the picture gallery.

There was something I wanted to know. 'Have you,' I asked, turning towards Sir William, 'Have you a portrait of your cousin Rupert, my...my...father?'

After an almost imperceptible hesitation he replied:

'No, I'm afraid not. As I told you earlier, he belonged to a distant branch of the family. The portraits we have in the gallery are all of people who have actually lived in the castle.'

'It was just that I saw—'

'You saw what?' Sir William's voice was sharp.

A bit worried as to what they might think of what to them might appear my slightly unorthodox behaviour, I told them of how in my search for fresh air I had come across the footman carrying a picture. 'There was something familiar about the young man's face, something that I couldn't place...'

'Yes?' The attention of both the Harfords was riveted upon me.

'Well,' I continued, a little disturbed at the effect my revelation was having upon them, 'I have since realised—oh, I know it is absurd really—but I have realised that the picture reminded me of myself...something about the eyes...' I looked from one to the other of them as I finished speaking; both wore a closed, guarded expression on their faces and I saw that Lady Marion was twisting nervously at her sash. Nicholas, I noticed, was watching them both closely.

Sir William smiled towards me, a forced, tight-lipped smile, 'And so you thought perhaps the picture was that of cousin Rupert, your father?'

'I didn't really think anything at all as concrete as that,' I objected, 'I was just curious...puzzled...nothing more.'

Sir William and Lady Marion looked at each other for a moment in silence. Then Sir William cleared his throat and said: 'I can see we shall have to be frank with you. The picture you saw was of my brother Rupert. We decided that it was better out of sight.'

'Your brother! But I don't understand...'
I began.

'Allow me to finish and then perhaps you will; I had a brother who...died when he was twenty; he and cousin Rupert were very much alike. They had the same eyes, the Harford eyes. You have them too and that is why the picture looked familiar.'

'But I still don't understand,' I persisted.

'I shall have to be more explicit then,' Sir William continued. 'As Marion and I have told you, we firmly believe you to be the child of our cousin Rupert Hanson; you resemble your father closely, but, and here is the trouble, you also resemble my brother very closely too and people might jump to the same erroneous conclusion as we ourselves did at first. My brother died unmarried and...'

I felt the hot colour rush to my cheeks as he went on: 'We had the picture removed to save embarrassment both to you and ourselves; as I have mentioned already, ours is an honoured name in Cornwall; we are a devout family and I will not have my brother's memory tarnished by gossip—'

'But such gossip could be roundly refuted, denounced as slander, could it not?' I demanded passionately.

'Indeed it could.' It was Nicholas who answered my outburst.

'But, I'm afraid, my child, that your reasoning betrays a lack of worldly experience. No matter how many times the gossip might be refuted, there would be those, and plenty of them who would be more than ready to believe it. Some of the mud always sticks.' He placed a comforting hand on my shoulder. 'Believe me, Carenza,' he said, and there was bitterness in his tone, 'I know.' He was looking directly at Lady Marion as he spoke and I saw that her gaze fell in the face of his level stare. For a moment or two there was a strained silence and then Sir William coughed nervously and muttered something to the effect that he was sure that everything would work out all right in the end and that sometimes people said things and then later regretted them. I had not the faintest notion what he was driving at but I got the impression that the others most certainly had. There was an undercurrent of feeling that was as positive as it was uncomfortable... On top of the confusion I was suffering on account of the story of the brother, it added to my bewilderment considerably. If only people would be completely sincere and honest and straightforward with each other I thought...

'This brother of yours, Harford,' it was Nicholas taking up the conversation again. 'May I ask whether he was older than yourself?' A sharp glance of understanding flashed between the two of them and I detected a slight note of triumph, I thought, in Sir William's voice as he replied: 'On the contrary, my dear Tangye, he was younger.'

'May I enquire how he met his death?' Again it was Nicholas speaking. There was a slight pause and then Sir William said flatly: 'He was drowned.'

Nicholas murmured his condolences politely and after thanking him Sir William suggested we get on with our tour.

Soon I could see that we were approaching the room that had had such a strange effect on me. Her hand on the knob, Lady Marion, eyes on her husband, hesitated before pushing the door open, an instant of time in which I too had noticed the barely perceptible nod of assent which Sir William had given her.

With my heart beating rapidly I followed

my hostess inside, conscious again of the disturbing feeling of familiarity, the nameless fear... There was a desk, but it was bare with an unused air to it that made me feel sad... Lady Marion was chattering brightly.

'Naturally a great many of the rooms in the castle are never used; this is one of them.'

I wanted to ask if Rupert Hanson had ever used the study while on a visit perhaps; it would explain the room's fascination for me a little if he had.

'Did your cousin Rupert ever stay in the castle on a visit, Lady Marion?' I asked abruptly.

'Never,' she answered. 'Why?'

'Oh, no special reason,' I said evasively. 'I just wondered, that was all.'

She looked at me searchingly, a puzzled expression in her dull eyes. Glancing towards Sir William I found that he too looked puzzled, and was watching me with a speculative air...I did my best to conceal from them the effect the study was having upon me, resisting the impulse to sit at the desk, to wander onto the balcony one minute, and run from the place the next...

'You are very pale, Carenza. Perhaps you would like to leave for home now?' Nicholas was beside me, a hand on my arm. His nearness set my pulses racing and I felt the colour rush to my cheeks.

'I am really perfectly all right again,' I murmured. 'I just felt a bit faint, that was all.'

'Well, your colour has come back now anyway,' intervened Lady Marion. 'Shall we get on? There is much of the castle you have not seen yet.'

During the remainder of the tour, a lot of what we saw, most of it, in fact, was lost upon me. My thoughts were half on the study and its effect on me, and half on Nicholas...of the thrill that had coursed through me at his touch...

It was time for us to leave.

'The kitchens and dungeons will have to wait for another day then,' smiled Sir William.

'You have dungeons?' I asked, surprised.

'Quite a number,' he replied. 'Nasty looking places...the sea creeps into some of them at high tide...'

A shiver ran through me as I wondered how many hapless prisoners had suffered in them in the past. We were making our way towards the great door that led outside.

'There is just one thing I would like to bring up before we leave,' Nicholas said suddenly.

'Yes?' Sir William's eyes, I thought, were wary.

'Would you have any objection,' went on Nicholas, 'to returning the locket to my wife? It is, after all, her property.'

There was a moment's strained silence before Sir William replied.

'Certainly Mrs Tangye may have the locket back if she so wishes. Will you please fetch it for her, Marion?'

Lady Marion went at once to do his bidding. She returned in less than two minutes, white-faced and empty-handed. 'It isn't there,' she whispered hoarsely to her husband.

'Not there?' Sir William's face had a pallor to match her own. 'And the letter, is that there?' There was a sense of urgency about his question that puzzled me greatly.

'No,' his wife told him. 'The letter too has vanished.'

'They were lying, of course.' We were in the carriage on our way back from the castle.

'About the locket?' I questioned Nicholas's statement. 'No, I do not agree, it was plain from their faces—'

'I do not mean about the locket,' cut in Nicholas impatiently. 'I mean all that rigmarole about their cousin—'

'My father?'

'Your father, or your alleged father to be more precise.'

'So you think...' I began slowly, the colour mounting my cheeks.

'I did not say that,' he broke in gently, 'but there was just something about the whole story which did not ring true. Although,' he went on reflectively, 'I have no doubt that the Harfords are desperately trying to convince both themselves and others that it is the truth.'

'Well, even if what you say is so,' I put in wearily, 'I could not find it in my heart to condemn them; the alternative is too hurtful, too distressing to contemplate; and after all, it is an explanation which could be true and one which brings relief and peace of mind not only to them but to me.'

'Then believe them my pretty one,' consoled Nicholas gently. 'If the story brings you comfort, believe it; I could be wrong.'

But you do not think you are, I concluded inwardly. Silence fell between us, a silence in which all manner of doubts and speculations crowded into my mind. Supposing Nicholas were right? What then? But he had to be wrong I told myself fiercely, unwilling to have my new found peace wrenched from me...

'I would very much like to have seen that locket.' Nicholas's voice broke in on my thoughts. 'Very much indeed.'

'So would I,' I agreed. 'It would have been nice to have had something of my mother's to keep...' My words trailed off as the scene when it was discovered that the locket was missing flashed before my eyes. The locket could have had no very great value I thought, either intrinsically or sentimentally for the Harfords, so why should the loss of it upset them so? Because I had no doubts whatever that it had upset them. True, there had been no mistaking the fact that they were relieved that Nicholas and I had been prevented from having it, but neither had there been any mistaking their fear.

It was all very confusing and puzzling

and I wondered if I should ever be able to be sure of the truth about myself. I closed my eyes wearily and lay back among the cushions. The thing to do, I told myself was to accept the story the Harfords had told me and stop speculating about them; the more I conjectured the more bewildered I should become. I glanced across the carriage at Nicholas. His eyes were closed but I knew that he was not asleep. The frown of concentration on his forehead told me that he was deep in thought. Was he still puzzling at the behaviour of the Harfords, I wondered, or did something of a more serious nature trouble him? Loving him as I did, I wished with all my heart that we were truly man and wife and that I could have shared his anxieties with him. Suddenly he opened his eyes and looked straight at me.

'Carenza—' there was a note in his voice I had not heard before.

'Yes?' I answered, my heart beating wildly.

He put out a hand as if to take mine, then let it fall back to his side. 'Nothing,' he said abruptly.

It took all my will power not to weep with disappointment.

CHAPTER 11

During the next few days Nicholas seemed to become more and more preoccupied and worried. He was curt and impatient even with Piram whom he obviously adored and with whom he was usually very gentle and understanding. The servants caught the rough side of his tongue on the slightest provocation and towards me he was distant and off-hand. I began to despair of his ever falling in love with me. That night in the carriage I had nursed a wild brief hope that perhaps in time...but in the face of his present coolness and indifference I chided myself at my foolishness in ever harbouring such an improbable dream.

Two things consoled me. One was the fact that he had never once referred to Lady Penelope again and the other was that he had said no more about going away.

I saw him rarely even so, for he was out practically the whole day, almost every day and I was usually in bed by the time he came back home. Several nights I heard him pacing the bedroom floor. I never asked him where he had been or what it was he had on his mind, although I longed with all my heart to know.

It was difficult sometimes to know how to spend my time.

I always looked in on Piram of course every day, but for the most part Jenny attended to the child's needs.

The little black pony which Nicholas had set aside for my use turned out to be a real blessing, and I took to riding out on the moor whenever the weather was suitable.

Besides filling in the empty hours which stretched before me, these rides in the peace and stillness did much to calm me when the burden of unrequited love seemed too heavy for me to bear.

On one such occasion I had become so engrossed in my thoughts, that it was with something of a start that I realised just how far I had ridden. I was within sight of Lady Penelope's establishment. I pulled my pony to a standstill and sat for a moment looking towards the house. I was on high ground and looking downwards, had a clear view of the back of the house itself and the courtyards.

Suddenly, a door opened and a man came into view. It was Nicholas and Lady Penelope was with him. They walked quickly across the courtyard, through an archway and passed out of my sight. My heart sank to the pit of my stomach at the sight of them together. I turned my pony's head for home, and tears of misery welling up in my eyes, galloped headlong over the moor. So this was where he spent his time. His attitude towards Lady Penelope *had* changed...and in the way I had suspected and feared...the fact that he did not mention her meant nothing...

Strangely enough he arrived home that night earlier than of late and inclined for once, to talk to me. He remarked upon my own silence and asked how I had spent my day.

'I went riding,' I told him shortly.

He gave me a quick glance. 'Where?'

'On the moor.'

'In which direction?'

'Towards Harris Point.' I did not look at him as I answered.

'Oh,' he said, surprise in his voice. 'It is really a wonder that I did not see you. I too have been in that neighbourhood today.'

I made no reply to this and kept my

eyes on my plate. I could feel that he was looking at me and sensed somehow that he was waiting for me to comment. When I did not do so, he went on: 'A message came early this morning, before you were down, from Penelope asking me to ride over if I could spare the time.'

'Oh yes,' I managed in a casual voice.

'It appears that she is having new buildings constructed on the Home Farm,' he informed me. 'And she wanted my advice.'

'Naturally!' I muttered angrily beneath my breath.

'What did you say?' There was a gleam in his eyes that I couldn't fathom. 'What was that?'

'Nothing,' I was in control of myself again.

'I said it was natural that she should seek your advice, that's all.' He looked at me thoughtfully through narrowed eyes but said no more on the subject. I was tempted to tell him that I had seen him at Harris Point but decided against it. He might conclude that I had been spying on him, I thought bitterly

Nicholas was speaking again. His voice, I felt, was too carefully casual.

'She will be riding over here in the morning, by the way; she would like to study the layout of the buildings here. I expect she will lunch with us so you had better inform Mrs Bray in plenty of time.'

'Very well,' I replied, steeling myself to keep my voice and manner cool and deliberate to hide the sinking feeling in my heart, 'I will see to it at once.'

I hardly slept at all that night. It seemed, I thought despairingly, that my suspicions were correct. Far from wishing to avoid the attentions of Lady Penelope as Nicholas had first led me to believe, he now appeared to welcome them...I dreaded the thought of the luncheon and wondered how on earth I should endure it. In desperation I asked if Piram could not be allowed, for once, to take a meal with us downstairs. I felt the child's presence might lessen the strain of the encounter and I was relieved and thankful when Nicholas agreed to my suggestion.

The situation, I think suited Lady Penelope as much as it did me; she devoted all her attention to the child (for the benefit of Nicholas, I thought bitterly) and was able to ignore me without being too blatantly impolite.

After luncheon I left the two of them to make a tour of the buildings Lady Penelope was interested in, while I went up to the nursery with Piram. It was a brisk, sunny day and I had promised to take him for a walk. We made our way towards the cliffs and when I saw that the tide was well out, decided to take the child down to the cove. The path was dry now and we made the descent without too much difficulty.

Piram was overjoyed to be able to run along the sands, and chattered excitedly all the time. It served to take my mind off Nicholas and Lady Penelope for a while as I joined in his games and helped him to search the rock-pools for shells and tiny fishes. He wanted to go into the caves but I would not let him. 'Another day,' I consoled him. 'The caves are very cold at this time of the year; wait until the summer comes.'

He accepted my ruling and did not persist. I had not been inside the caves myself since that first time I had come across the heap of salt. Funnily enough I had thought little about the matter, other more momentous issues having pushed it to the far recesses of my mind. But now that I thought about it again I decided that one day, before too long, I would follow the cave to its full extent and find out where it led to if I could.

Piram was tiring. We made our way home. As we passed by a group of buildings which adjoined the outer courtyard, I wondered if Nicholas and Lady Penelope were anywhere about, but there were no signs of them.

After I had taken the child back to his nurse I went downstairs to the drawing-room to ring for tea. On my way there I had to pass the door of Nicholas's study; it was very, very slightly ajar and I heard voices. Nicholas and Lady Penelope were talking in low tones; I had no intention to eavesdrop but their words came clearly to me. With all my heart I wished they had not.

'How much longer do you think it will take you?' It was Lady Penelope speaking.

My heart almost bursting I waited for Nicholas to answer her. 'Not very long now, I assure you. But why on earth didn't you come to me sooner—was it pride?'

'Yes.' Penelope's voice was quieter than I had ever heard it.

'But you must have known that I...'

I did not wait to hear more. Putting my hands over my ears I hurried away as fast as I could.

Never until I die shall I know how I got through tea that afternoon. Nicholas and Penelope behaved as if nothing were amiss and somehow I managed to do likewise. My face felt stiff with the effort of smiling and talking normally, but at last the ghastly charade came to a close and Lady Penelope left us.

There was something I knew I had to say to Nicholas. I wasted no time. As soon as we had seen Lady Penelope off, I took a tight grip on myself and in as controlled a manner as I could, asked if he would mind retiring to the drawing-room for a minute. He followed me inside. 'Well?' he asked looking at me questioningly.

I turned away from the devastating sea-blue eyes. My back towards him I said slowly: 'If ever you wish to end our...our marriage, Nicholas, I will not oppose you; it could very easily be annulled.'

A deathly silence followed my words. It went on so long that I turned eventually to look at him. There was an unfathomable expression on his face. 'I am, and always have been, perfectly aware of that,' he said calmly and walked out of the room. Unseeing, I stared after him, clinging to the only comfort I had, the dignity of having let him know that I would never seek to hold him against his will.

The next morning when I came down for breakfast there was no sign of Nicholas. As this had been the case several times of late I did not feel at all perturbed about it. Then I saw the letter beside my plate. I felt myself go cold and clutched hold of the back of the chair for support. So it had come. He wished to be free of me...with trembling hands I slit open the square white envelope and read the bold, well formed script. A heartfelt sigh of relief escaped me.

The letter was merely to tell me that he had gone to the south coast on business; it would depend on how things went as to exactly how long he would be away. The letter was brief and to the point; it was signed: *Nicholas*. As I laid it down upon the table I realised that I was shaking all over. There was no reference whatever in the letter to what I had said to him the night before, nor was there the slightest hint of warmth or even friendliness. It was cold, formal and completely impersonal. As on the night my grandmother had died, a sudden swift despair engulfed me.

Did he, I wondered bitterly, really intend to return? And if he did, would it not be solely on account of Piram...

When Mrs Bray came into the room to clear away the breakfast things I was still sitting hunched despondently over the table, staring broodingly into my empty coffee cup. At once I straightened myself up and tried to appear as though everything were perfectly alright with me. I did not want her to suspect the bitterness of my thoughts, the longing to be with Nicholas, but I do not think for one moment that I deceived her. After giving me a shrewd glance she remarked how lucky I was that the master was considerate enough not to expect me to go with him on his journeys and spend my time 'rattling over bumpy roads.' She asked what plans I had for the day. Up to that moment I had had none, but I decided I must enter into the spirit of her little charade.

'I think I shall go down to the cove,' I said brightly, 'there is a cave there that I would like to explore.'

' 'Tis a good idea,' she beamed, 'but be careful, and stick to the proper path down the cliffs,' a serious look crossed her face. 'We want no more nasty accidents.' Idly wondering what she could be referring to I promised to be very careful.

When I reached the cliffs I saw Mrs Polglaze walking along the path. Even from behind, there was no mistaking her ungainly bulk. It was a good day for walking and I did not attach any significance to her being there.

The state of the tide was just right for my purpose. It was on its way out, leaving a wide enough stretch of hard, damp sand for me to skirt the foot of the cliffs without difficulty. And there would be plenty of time for my exploration without the least danger of being cut off.

A mild excitement filled me as I began my adventure. I had not gone more than a few yards inside the cave however, when I sensed that I was not alone. I stiffened, a finger of fear crawling up my spine, and was on the point of beating a hasty retreat when the mad woman suddenly appeared in front of me.

'I've been waiting for you to come again,'

she announced before I could recover from my surprise.

She looked wild and unkempt as on the day I had seen her on the moor.

'Waiting for me to come again?' I echoed, 'whatever do you mean?'

'You came here before,' she cried, a sly look in her eyes. 'I saw you.'

'But I didn't see you,' I gasped. 'I saw no-one.'

'Oh,' she explained, 'I kept hidden until I knew who it was and then when I saw it was you, you ran away.'

She laughed then loudly, peal after peal of the maniacal laughter I had heard twice before. In spite of my nervousness I was curious as to what had brought her to the cave. Making my voice as calm and as friendly as I could I asked her what she was doing.

'This is my secret place,' she giggled. 'It is where I keep all my treasures.'

'Your treasures?'

She ignored my question. 'They'll never find them here,' she muttered. 'They think they're clever you know,' she went on turning towards me knowingly. 'But they're not as clever as me.'

I decided it would be best to humour her.

'No, indeed,' I murmured in agreement.

'It's very pretty,' she announced suddenly. 'I like it.'

I didn't know what to say to this piece of information so I kept silent.

'I saw them put it away after you'd gone. Would you like to see it?'

It suddenly dawned on me what she was babbling about. I forgot my fear of her. 'The locket!' I cried out excitedly. 'You have found my locket—'

'It's mine,' she broke in angrily, her eyes wild.

'Yes, yes of course,' I placated her. 'It is yours for sure; but I would dearly love to see it. I'm so glad you found it.'

'They didn't know I was watching them,' she went on. 'They never know. I'm very quiet you see. They never know where I am.' She leaned closer to me and whispered in a conspiratorial voice: 'They think I'm mad you know!'

Without giving me chance to make any comment she continued. 'Why didn't you come home sooner, you silly girl?'

'Where from?' I asked in consternation.

'From Germany of course,' she answered impatiently.

'But I have never been—' I began, then

218

stopped. Mad people did not like to be contradicted I had once heard. 'I had to wait until I had money for the voyage,' I improvised quickly.

'Such nonsense,' she retorted. 'Come, it isn't far. Follow me.'

She walked further inside the cave and I followed closely behind her. After a minute or so she stopped and began peering closely at the walls of rock on either side of her. She soon found what she was looking for and carefully removed what I saw were two loose pieces of rock lodged in the wall on her right. Behind them was a small cavity. Her clawlike fingers darted into it. A smile of triumph covered her face as she turned towards me, the little silver locket gleaming in her outstretched palm. My heart began to beat quickly.

'May I look inside it please?' I asked coaxingly.

'Of course you may, stupid,' she replied.

Reverently I held the tiny bauble in my hands. My mother's locket. The only thing in the world belonging to her that I should ever see or touch. And at last I was to see the face of my father... Gently I prised the locket open and gasped in amazement at the picture that met my eyes. For the face in my mother's locket was the same face that I had seen in the picture at Fistral Castle. The picture they had said was of Sir William's brother.

'Who is it?' I asked urgently. 'Tell me please, do you know who it is?'

'Of course I do,' she laughed wildly. 'It's Rupert.'

'Yes, but which one?' I asked urgently. 'Sir William's brother or his cousin?' I broke off before the incredulous expression on her face.

'There was only one Rupert,' she announced flatly. Obviously she had never heard of Rupert Hanson. It would be useless to question her further. She would not be able to shed any light on the mystery. I peered at the small picture once more. Certainly Sir William had told me how very much alike the two Ruperts were. But I had not imagined for one moment that the resemblance would be so striking.

'He was drowned, you know.' There was a pathetic sadness about the mad woman's voice as she spoke.

'Who was drowned?' I asked.

'Rupert of course,' she replied. 'Didn't anybody tell you?' Before I could answer this strange question she continued, 'He should never have gone out in the boat that day. Anybody could see it was too rough. But he was fearless. I don't think he ever saw danger in anything...'

She broke off as if the trend of thought had escaped her. Since I could not make any sense at all of what she was talking about I seized the opportunity to say that it was time I was going home. She looked at me vaguely, as if she had forgotten who I was. Then a sort of glazed look came into her eyes.

'He had a secret place too,' she announced suddenly.

'Who had?'

'Rupert of course.' Her tone was impatient. 'I know where it is.'

'Where?' I asked.

She ignored my question and looked at me for several moments in silence. She seemed to be making her mind up about something. 'I like you,' she said at length. 'I think you're kind.'

'Thank you very much,' I murmured, wondering what she was leading up to.

She came and stood very close to me and took the locket from my hand. Shaking her head from side to side she said: 'You can't have it; it's mine you see and I like it.'

I turned towards the way out. 'Goodbye,' I called. 'I really must be going home now.'

'Wait!' She gripped my arm in a vice-like grip. 'I'll show you *his* secret place if you like.' She still held my arm and her eyes glared wildly into mine. I began to feel afraid again.

'Another day perhaps,' I told her gently. 'It truly is time that I started for home.'

She was still holding the locket. Suddenly she let go of me and pointing to my mother's name engraved upon it, touched the word *Elaine*. 'It says *that* on it.'

'Yes,' I nodded. 'I see that it does.'

'It says it on Rupert's treasure,' her eyes were dreaming again. 'I've seen it.'

I forgot my fear in a moment. Could it be that she had found something else belonging to my mother...

'What is Rupert's treasure?' I asked excitedly. There was a long pause before she spoke again. And when she did it was as if she talked to herself not to me.

'It isn't pretty,' she muttered. 'I don't see why he wanted it for a treasure. A piece of paper. Not pretty like mine.' And she stroked the little silver locket lovingly before returning it carefully to the cavity in the wall.

I was torn with indecision about her. Had she, I wondered, somehow stumbled upon a letter written either to or by my mother, or was it merely the ramblings of a sick mind? If only I could be sure. And if she had found a letter how on earth had it come to be at the castle? Suddenly I made up my mind.

'I would like to see Rupert's treasure,' I told her.

'It's not here,' she said with a wild laugh, 'it's there,' and darted further inside the cave and out of my sight.

I stared after her, chiding myself for having for one moment taken her seriously. Remembering my reason for coming to the cave I set off after her. It seemed obvious now that there was another entrance to it and that she was heading towards it. I could hear her stumbling along in front of me as the cave grew darker. Soon the ground started to rise slightly and shafts of light penetrated the gloom. I could see the madwoman again now, she was just beginning to climb up a narrow flight of steps; she did not once look round behind her and seemed entirely oblivious of my presence.

When I reached the top of the stairway and pushed my way out through the mass of undergrowth and scrub which concealed the entrance, I was just in time to see her running across the moor towards a clump of trees some fifty yards away. A pony was tethered there. She sprang up onto its back and galloped off over the moor. I looked about me curiously and was surprised to find that I was no great distance from Trenance House. I tried to straighten up my dishevelled appearance a little and set off home, my emotions tumultuous. It had moved me deeply holding my mother's locket, seeing my father's face, and tears pricked my eyes as I thought longingly of how wonderful it would have been had they still been alive...

A sound broke my reverie. I looked up to see a carriage rumbling along over the track towards me. As it passed by me I thought I glimpsed Lady Penelope's face through one of the windows but I could not be sure. It was certainly a splendid affair and seemed to have come from the direction of Trenance House.

I wondered angrily if she had been to

call and then dismissed the idea since I was sure she would not dream of visiting in Nicholas's absence. That she would know of his absence seemed certain in my mind. He would be sure to confide in her I thought bitterly. As I walked through the courtyard I came across young Bray. I asked him if Lady Tresidder had called.

'No, Mrs Tangye,' he answered. 'I did see the carriage though ma'am, along the cliff tops; Lady Penelope be talking through the window with old Mrs Polglaze.' I dismissed the lad's words without so much as a second thought. At the time there seemed no reason to do otherwise. In any case my mind was too full of the events of the afternoon for me to dwell upon anything else. It had been so wonderful to hold my mother's locket, to have that one brief link with her...but I was still wracked with uncertainty about my true identity. Now that I had seen the face in the locket it seemed to me almost certain that it was the same face as in the picture at the castle, that it was Rupert Harford...and that therefore I was a bastard after all... No wonder that Nicholas was now regretting his hasty marriage. I was a nobody and it was true that I could ruin him socially as

Lady Penelope had said. It had been stupid of me ever to hope that he might come to love me as I had come to love him... My despair in that moment was so great as to almost overwhelm me. Dejectedly I made my way indoors and went at once upstairs to my room.

Next morning when I went up to the nursery, Jenny was in a chatty mood. It appeared she had seen old Mrs Polglaze talking with Lady Penelope the day she had lunched with us.

'You should have seen her ma'am,' she said indignantly. 'All smiles she was, and "yes mi lady", and "no mi lady", and her as sulky and grumpy as can be with everybody here.'

It was not for me to discuss one servant with another. I made some non-committal rejoinder. Jenny was undeterred. 'She gave her something as well, ma'am; I couldn't make out what it was 'cos Mrs Polglaze put it in her pocket quick, but I heard her say, "Thank you mi lady, 'tis an honour to serve you I'm sure." '

'Well,' I replied, 'Perhaps Mrs Polglaze had done some small errand for Lady Penelope and was being rewarded.'

Actually I was puzzled by what the girl had told me but had no intention of revealing the fact.

'Mind, she is a great lady,' went on Jenny, 'with her fine clothes and her beauty. No wonder she be always going to balls and the like in all the great houses—going to one in Penzance she is, this very week, John says—'

The girl broke off suddenly, covering her mouth with her hand in a confused, embarrassed fashion. Penzance! On the south coast...where Nicholas was...

I did not let Jenny see the effect her words had on me. Calmly I asked, 'John; who is he?'

'Lady Penelope's coachman,' Jenny said in a rush.

'He be sweet on me ma'am...' She blushed and giggled looking coy and bashful.

'I see!' I smiled. So that was how Jenny had come to be in the courtyard and seen Lady Penelope with Mrs Polglaze. She and the coachman had evidently seized on the opportunity of spending a bit of time together alone somewhere. I wondered what else they might have seen or heard.

I left the nursery abruptly, anxious to

be alone, and sought the sanctuary of my bedroom. I walked through the room and went and stood as I often did when I felt miserable, on the little balcony which faced the front courtyard. I was just about to lean dejectedly against the wooden railings surrounding it when my bedroom door burst open and little Piram hurled himself across the room and straight towards me. He grabbed the wooden spirals close to the bottom, trying to climb up them. I grabbed him as he fell and a section of the railings crashed on to the courtyard below.

Crying with fright and shock, he clung to me as I cradled him in my arms endeavouring to comfort him. I carried him back to the nursery and put him straight to bed, admonishing Jenny roundly for having let the child run from the nursery. 'If I hadn't been there he would have been killed,' I scolded her. The poor girl was full of remorse and on the verge of tears. My anger lessened a little. 'Well do try to watch him more carefully,' I said more kindly, placing a hand on her shoulder. 'If anything happened to him I tremble to think what his father would say.'

'Me too, ma'am,' she sniffed.

I returned to my room and sat down. Now that it was all over I shook from head to foot. It was not only from shock. I had leaned my full weight on those railings only the day before and they had been as firm as a rock. Someone had tampered with them while I was out of the house... Someone had intended me to crash on to the courtyard below...little Piram by his mischievousness had probably saved my life... As far as I knew there was but one person who bore me a grudge, and that was Mrs Polglaze, but I did not think that even she hated me enough to wish to harm me. I did not know what to do about the matter and wished with all my heart that Nicholas were at home. It occurred to me that I could ask the other servants if they had seen any unauthorized person entering or leaving my room, but felt that such a course would inevitably lead to suspicion and gossip between them. The railings would have to be repaired though.

I went downstairs to the housekeeper and instructed her to see to it that one of the estate workmen mended them right away. When she remarked that the railings were probably rotten through age, I did not argue with her. If anyone were trying to harm me, better to let whoever it was think that I was unsuspecting, I decided; in that way I might the more easily discover who it was.

When I went to bed that night I locked the door on to the landing. Then I opened the door into Nicholas's room, went inside and locked his door onto the landing, thus making doubly sure I was safe. I left the communicating door open for once, wishing it could always be so...

When I awoke the next morning it was a dismal world that confronted me. A sea fret had come in with the tide and lay over everything like a wet, cold blanket. It was impossible to see barely a few yards. At intervals I could hear the mournful boom of the fog horn sounding its warning note out to sea. Already nervy and tense after the railings episode, the gloom of the morning served to make me more so. I wondered how on earth I should get through the day if the fog did not lift. There was no question of taking Piram for his customary outing so I played with him in the nursery for an hour or so instead. After lunch I settled myself before the library fire to read, glad, perhaps more than I had ever been, that my grandmother had instilled in me a love of books.

It was about half-past three in the afternoon when the fog lifted, and I decided to go out. Even when it was cold I loved to walk along the cliff tops, and there was rarely a day that I did not do so. The sea in all its moods held an irresistible fascination for me. I ran upstairs to put on my cloak, pausing on my way out to go to the kitchens to tell Mrs Bray that I would take tea half an hour later than usual. Mrs Polglaze, I noticed, was busy at the stone sink. She did not look up.

The absence of any wind warned me of the danger of the possible return of the fog, but I was so restless and sick of being inside that I paid no heed.

I had been walking for perhaps twenty minutes or so when it began to descend again. I turned round at once, deeming it expedient to get back to Trenance House without delay. It was when I was about half-way back that I heard the footsteps. The fog had come down again like a blanket now, and I could see no-one.

I called out: 'Is anyone there?' but there was no answer; only the screeching of the seagulls and the crashing of the waves at the foot of the cliffs. Thinking that I must have been imagining things I walked on again. The footsteps followed. Terror rose within me. Someone had tried to kill me once, why not again? I was small and slight, easy to drag to the cliff edge... Fear galvanized me into action I left the path and ran away from the cliffs. I knew that I could not be far from the point where the track turned inland, towards the house but I did not dare to remain on it for another second. Better to get lost than be pushed to my death in the boiling sea.

But fortune was with me. I had run only a short distance when I came upon one of the estate workers. He had been attending to the palisade round the deer park, he told me. Even in the mist he made his way unerringly towards the house. 'Have you been on the cliff path at all?' I asked him.

'No, Mrs Tangye.' His voice held surprise at my question. 'The deer park be away from the cliffs.'

'Yes of course,' I murmured. 'Stupid of me.'

He looked at me uneasily. When we reached the big iron gates he touched his cap and vanished in the direction of the stables and outbuildings.

As I crossed one of the inner courtyards I met old Mrs Polglaze coming from the opposite direction. She had on her outdoor clothing.

'Where have you been?' I asked sharply.

She gave me a hostile look. 'Only to the store-house,' she muttered and indicated the basket of potatoes she carried.

I said no more and went on my way along the yard. I had an uneasy feeling that the woman was lying; her clothes, I had noticed, were as damp as my own. They would not have become so from a visit to the store-house. Where had she been? Could it have been along the cliff path?

I was just about to enter the house when I heard someone coming up behind me. I turned sharply. It was Nicholas. 'I thought you were on the South Coast,' I gasped.

'I arrived home some while ago,' he replied shortly, 'Just after, as Mrs Bray informed me, you had been so foolish as to set out for a walk.' I blushed at the criticism.

'But you yourself have obviously been out in the fog,' I defended myself, 'Your cloak is as wet as mine.'

'I came to look for you,' came the reply. 'But missed you somehow.'

'I left the cliff path.' I told him. 'I... I thought it might be dangerous...' I did not intend to tell him about the footsteps for fear he thought I was being fanciful again. For a moment he looked at me with a slightly disbelieving frown as if he sensed that I was keeping something back, but all he said was: 'Very sensible, Carenza.'

CHAPTER 12

It was on the very next day that I learned about the murder. After breakfast I went up in my usual way, to the nursery. I found the place in an uproar. Jenny, in tears, was stuffing her clothes into a valise while Mrs Bray stood over her, scolding and upbraiding the girl in no uncertain terms. Plainly fascinated, Piram was staring at the pair of them in bewilderment.

'Whatever is going on?' I asked in astonishment. They both began to answer me at the same time. I held up my hand. 'Please! Now, Jenny, what is the matter; why are you crying and why are you packing your things—?'

'I'm frightened, ma'am.' The girl sobbed. 'I'm not staying in this 'ouse another minute—'

'Such rubbish,' snorted Mrs Bray indignantly. 'I've told you girl the old woman only wants to be rid of you; she thinks she'll get back up here if she frightens you away.'

I began to see what had happened. 'Mrs Polglaze has told you about the ghost, Jenny, is that it?'

She nodded.

'Have you either seen or heard it?'

'No, ma'am.'

'But you believe there is one?'

The girl nodded, her eyes round with fear.

'Mrs Polglaze says as how it's *her*, ma'am; says she can't rest, poor soul... coming tapping on the window like she do...'

'A lot of nonsense,' put in Mrs Bray roundly. 'And I'm ashamed that a niece of mine should be so stupid as to believe it.' She gave the poor nursemaid an impatient glower.

'Don't be too hard on her, Mrs Bray,' I interrupted. 'She is not the only one to have believed the story, remember, and young as she is, it is not surprising that she should be upset and afraid.' I turned to Jenny. 'I am fairly certain,' I told her, 'that I have hit upon the explanation of the ghost story. When you hear it you will see that there is nothing to fear.'

I then went on to tell them both the conclusion I had reached; it had come to me when I met the mad woman in the cave. She was the ghost; everyone knew she roamed the moor at all hours, and tapping on a window pane was just the sort of stupid behaviour she might indulge in; but she was harmless.

'She couldn't suddenly disappear, like the ghosts do,' interrupted Jenny.

I smiled. 'I think she could,' I corrected, and went on to tell them about the moorland exit to the beach cave. 'She could easily run down the steps and from here it would look as though she had vanished into thin air.'

'That's as maybe, ma'am,' argued the girl stolidly, 'but what about the murder?'

'Murder?' I gasped. 'What murder?'

'Hold your tongue, Jenny,' Mrs Bray was on her feet. 'If you want to leave, go; and let's not have any more mischief done than's been done already.' She made as if to hustle the girl from the room at once, but I stopped her. There was obviously more to the girl's fears than I knew about.

'Do you know this story of murder?' I asked Mrs Bray. 'If so, I wish to hear it.' I glanced at Piram. 'But not in front of the child.' I turned to Jenny. 'Perhaps you will remain for ten minutes while your aunt and I talk?' The girl nodded in assent and Mrs Bray and I repaired to my room. There I heard the story.

Nicholas's first wife had died in extremely mysterious circumstances: she had gone to her death in a fall from the top of the cliffs one foggy night; it had not been easy to determine whether some of the marks on her body had been caused by the fall or by a struggle...but there had been no concrete evidence against anybody. Even so, ugly rumours had started, rumours that it was her husband who had pushed her to her death, rumours all too easy to believe in when it was suggested that Mrs Tangye had had a lover...

'She got no more than she deserved,' the little housekeeper insisted. 'But I'll never believe the master had anything to do with it.'

'Nor I,' I began and stopped as the events of the last two or three days flashed before my eyes; the broken railings...he could have tampered with them before he went away...the footsteps in the fog...they could have been his...

Oh, God, I agonized inwardly, don't let it be him, anyone but him...

Mrs Bray was peering at me anxiously: 'Are you all right, ma'am, you be white as the clay.'

With a tremendous effort of will I pulled myself together. 'Yes,' I said, and my voice sounded strange even in my own ears. 'Yes, I'm all right; but I'm tired suddenly, and I would like to be alone for a while.'

Looking at me searchingly, the house-keeper withdrew. For minutes I remained motionless where I sat, my mind in torment. What was I to do? Surely Nicholas would never be so desperate as to murder me. I had told him I would go away whenever he wished it. But if he had already killed...things that had puzzled me came flashing into my mind: Lady Marion's words about if I ever needed help... Lady Penelope saying that Nicholas had made yet a second mistake...that he would live to regret his impulsive behaviour...and nobody could deny that he was impulsive; look at the way he had proposed to me...impulsive and possessed of a mighty temper...the sort of man who might act first and think afterwards...I got up from my chair and began to pace the room in my agitation; perhaps he had been driven to murder...well I would see that he was not driven to it a second time; I would leave as quickly as possible. Then I upbraided myself for being so ready to believe the worst of him. Nothing had been proved. It was rumour, ugly rumour, set about perhaps by an enemy...

'Some of the mud always sticks.' How bitterly he had said the words to Lady Marion that day. Obviously she had believed the worst of him; it seemed that Lady Penelope did also...she had hinted right from the beginning and this was what it was all about; I had been wrong in thinking she meant the ghost story... But if she believed him a murderer why did she pursue him? Could it be I wondered, that she merely used the rumours, as far as she dare, just to frighten me and upset me and didn't really believe them herself... Oh, it was all so puzzling and distressing and involved... I just didn't know what to think, what to believe... But the cold hard fact remained that attempts had been made on my life; it was imperative that I should leave Trenance House.

Suddenly a picture flashed before my mind; the scene at the inn and the two girls discussing me; what had the second one said? I couldn't recall exactly but I knew that it was something to the effect that I wouldn't be staying long if I had any sense...all these things began to add up, each one a mystery to me no longer. But how to get away. I could not go to Nicholas and tell him bluntly that I was leaving him; that I was afraid for my life, that someone, I knew not whom, was trying to kill me...

I still could not wholly believe that it was Nicholas. Although I felt sure that he now regretted his hasty marriage, he could be rid of me without resorting to murder...but whoever it was I must leave, and leave quickly.

After thinking the matter over carefully I hit upon a plan. I schooled myself to behave naturally, and then immediately after luncheon I asked Nicholas if he had any objections to my going to the Harfords the following day.

He seemed, I thought, a little surprised at my suggestion but said pleasantly: 'None at all, go by all means if you wish; it just so happens that I have to make a visit to Newquay tomorrow so you will be able to come along with me as far as Fistral Castle as I shall be passing close by it.'

Mention of the word Newquay reminded me that I had not told him about Jenny. No amount of pleading either by myself or her aunt had changed her mind for her; she had left the minute I had returned to the nursery earlier in the day. I did not tell Nicholas the whole truth, I'm afraid; all I said was that she had heard about the ghost and had gone.

The outburst of anger I had expected from him did not come; all he did was to pass a hand over his forehead and say wearily: 'It is no more than I expected.'

'Will you be taking Piram to Newquay with you?' I asked. 'There will be no one to attend to him except Mrs Bray.'

'No,' came the prompt reply. 'It would be highly inconvenient; unless you take him with you yourself, Mrs Bray will have to leave her other duties and look after him for the day.' He looked at me questioningly as he spoke and I could not meet his eyes as I replied: 'I don't think it would be a advisable for him to accompany me this time...I may decide to stay late...for the night even...' I rose from my chair as I went on: 'I will go at once and make arrangements with Mrs Bray.' As I left the room hurriedly I could feel his gaze following me...

I found Mrs Bray in the kitchen and told her my plans. Mrs Polglaze was there, busy at the sink; something told me that she was listening intently to every word I said.

★ ★ ★ ★

I did not sleep at all that night. The morning found me heavy-eyed and wretched. My pillow was wet with the tears of misery which had overwhelmed me during those long, dark hours. I got out of bed grimly determined to resign myself to the path I had set out for myself. I would go to Fistral Castle and from there I would make my way to the coaching inn and after that the south coast and Lord Tregonning's home.

He had promised me that I could serve in his household if I wished to do so at any time; and that time had arrived. At first I

242

thought of putting on the clothes in which I had come to Trenance House in the first place, but I changed my mind, knowing that such behaviour might cause Nicholas to suspect something. I could return these expensive clothes which he had bought for me, later on, I decided; I did not consider that I had any right to them now...

A surprise awaited me when I got downstairs. A letter had come—a messenger had, it seemed, handed it to Mrs Polglaze, a letter from Lady Marion inviting me to go and see her that very day; she had something important to discuss with me, the letter said, and she would be very gratified if I could humour her by paying a visit at such short notice. Dejectedly I wondered what it could be she wished to talk about; whatever it was it would be of little consequence to me now...

'A clear case of telepathy,' announced Nicholas. 'Do you not agree?'

I murmured my assent.

In the carriage he remarked on my quietness. I said that I was tired and had slept rather badly. He looked at me keenly for a moment but made no further comment. I was glad that he had not come up to the nursery that morning.

Saying goodbye to little Piram had upset me dreadfully and all the more because I had had to conceal my emotion both from the child himself and from the watchful eyes of Mrs Bray. The effort of holding back my feelings imposed a tremendous strain and I was relieved when we reached the castle. I watched the carriage until it was out of sight and this time I let the tears fall; there was no one to see or to care, never would be ever again I reminded myself bitterly as I strained my eyes for a last glimpse of the man I loved...

Pulling myself together I made my way to the castle and was shown at once into the morning room. I gasped in surprise when I saw who awaited me there; it was Lady Penelope. She hastened to explain the absence of Lady Marion and her own presence.

'Marion has been unexpectedly called away and asked if I would play hostess in her absence; she would very much like you to wait, and expects to be home before dinner.' She smiled at me charmingly as she spoke and showed none of her old animosity.

I was at a loss to know how to behave. On the one hand I had no wish to spend several hours in Lady Penelope's company, but on the other, I was very curious to find out what it was that Lady Marion wished to speak to me about; I nursed a hope, frail though it was, that she might have found out something more regarding my father or mother.

Lady Penelope was speaking again: 'It was fortunate that I decided to call on Marion today, wasn't it? It could have been extremely awkward for her otherwise.'

'Yes,' I murmured. 'Yes, indeed.'

'You will stay and wait then?' Her smile was honeysweet. 'Come, sit here by the fire. I will ring for someone to take your cloak.'

'I will wait for a while at least,' I told her doing as she bid; 'I am anxious to see Lady Marion and have made arrangements to be away from home all day as it happens.' In spite of the agreeable way in which she was behaving I still did not trust my companion and had no intention of confiding my real intentions to her.

The afternoon passed pleasantly enough. Lady Penelope asked if I had seen round the castle and when I replied that I had seen only part of it, offered to show me the rest. Her manner remained friendly and in spite of her past unpleasantness I began to wonder if I might have misjudged her a little. When at half past three, Lady Harford had still not returned, I expressed my desire to leave. It would soon drop in dark and I wanted to be well on my way to the inn before that happened; there was, I thought, no question now of my staying the night, with the Harfords away. But Lady Penelope clearly did not want me to leave.

'Marion will be *so* disappointed,' she argued, 'and you did say that you had made arrangements to be away all day, didn't you?'

'But soon it will be dark...' I began.

'And what of it?' she countered. 'The Harfords will send you home in their coach, or indeed you could share mine if you so desired.'

There was nothing more I could say. My state of mind was such that I did not really care where I was, or what I did...life, bleak and meaningless stretched before me...I might just as well spend another hour or so in this woman's company as anywhere else...

After tea Lady Penelope suggested that I might like to rest a while before dinner.

She took me upstairs into one of the guest rooms. 'Marion and William are bound to return in time for dinner,' she affirmed, 'And I am going to take it upon myself to give instructions to the staff to that effect; I will see you later on, shall we say about six-thirty.' And with that she withdrew.

Lying on the bed and looking round the vast bedroom it became obvious to me that my sojourn there had been expected; the heavy velvet curtains had been drawn against the night, the lamps on the dressing-table had been lit, and hot water and towels provided. I frowned. I had been with Lady Penelope all afternoon and she had never given any orders to have this room prepared for me. She must have issued the instructions before I arrived; but how did she know that I was coming...for the first time a faint feeling of unease began to stir in me, but before I could make up my mind what to do about it, the handle on my door started to turn very slowly.

I sat up in alarm, a nameless dread flooding through me. Terrified I watched with helpless fascination as the door opened slowly inwards. A figure stood silhouetted in the doorway.

It was the madwoman. In the light

of the flickering candle she carried she looked even more grotesque than usual. Yet strangely, on seeing her, much of my fear left me. I had an instinctive assurance that she meant me no harm. She peered carefully up and down the corridor before entering the room, a finger to her lips. Seemingly satisfied that she had not been observed, she closed the door quietly behind her and came and stood close to my bed. Her voice was a thin rasp of a whisper. 'I saw the light,' she began.

'But how on earth did you know that I was here at all?' I asked. 'I'm quite sure you were nowhere to be seen when I arrived at the castle.'

She smiled the half-mad, sly smile I had come to know well. 'I see everything,' she whispered knowingly. 'But come, I have come to show you Rupert's treasure.'

'Are you really sure that you wish me to see it?' I hedged, remembering the outcome of our previous conversation on the matter.

'Yes,' she replied fiercely. 'You see I want you to have it.' She paused a moment, a far away look in the bewildered eyes. 'I would have let you have the locket, but it's so pretty...' She looked at me pathetically, her head on one side as though seeking reassurance.

'You keep it,' I said gently. 'I don't mind at all.' As I spoke I was getting off the bed and pulling on my wrap.

She herself was enveloped in a coarse linen smock with a red shawl knotted about her shoulders; her feet were bare, her hair matted and unkempt. I followed her along the seemingly never-ending corridors wondering where she was taking me.

There were no doubts in my mind at all as to what would ensue: it would turn out to be a wild-goose chase. But I felt I must humour her, my heart consumed with pity for the poor deranged creature. How very terrible the lot of the half mad, I reflected, torn and tortured by a mass of fantasies from which they can never be free. What a bewildering world of shadows they inhabit. I wondered what had happened to make this poor creature as she was. Had she been born to it, or had some wounding experience of life proved too much for her to bear?

So intent was I on my thoughts that I had not taken particular notice of where we were heading. It was with a gasp of surprise that I saw that we were outside the door of the little study, the room that had affected me so strangely. Again the madwoman peered up and down the corridor before entering. She closed the door quietly and beckoned me to follow her to the desk. Giving me the candle to hold she began to open the desk, pulling out drawers and feeling inside with her thin, gnarled fingers. Her eyes held a feverish look and I felt a surge of excitement run through me. Had she really found something with my mother's name on it? Could this be the reason for the room's hold upon me, a hold felt more strongly each time I entered...?

Suddenly she gave a snort of satisfaction. 'Ah,' she breathed, 'I have it.' I heard a faint click at the back of the drawer she was groping inside and caught my breath as she triumphantly revealed a letter.

'There,' she cried, thrusting it into my hands. 'Read it. I will hold the candle for you.'

With shaking fingers I pulled the thick, folded paper out of the unsealed envelope. *'My dearest Elaine,'* I read. *'My own darling little German wife, how I miss you. I will return for you as soon as...'*

The words swam and blurred in front of

me so that I could not see them properly. Through the tears of joy which filled my eyes and streamed down my face I made out the signature at the bottom: *'Your devoted husband Rupert.'*

I looked at the envelope. It was addressed to Mrs Rupert Harford at an address in Germany. I was so utterly overjoyed at my discovery that at first I did not fully take in the words. I read them again a second time. 'Mrs Rupert Harford.' I said the name wonderingly. 'Harford, *not* Hanson...'

So I *was* Rupert Harford's child. Nicholas had always suspected so...the Harfords too, I believed...but he had *not* died unmarried as Sir William had stated; he and my mother must have married in secret...the tears flowing down my face unrestrainedly I began to read the letter again... It was at that moment that a shadow fell across the page. I looked up to find Lady Penelope beside me. There was a look in her eyes I could not fathom.

'I came to call you for dinner,' she said, 'as you were not in your room I began to look for you—'

'Look,' I interrupted her ecstatically, 'Look what the madwoman has found,

Lady Penelope, a letter from my father—' I stopped before the look of blinding hatred which filled her face.

'I'm afraid,' she said, and the menace in her voice was deadly, 'who your father was or whether you were born in or out of wedlock can only be of academic interest now.'

I looked at her in alarm, fear replacing my joyous tears. 'Why, Lady Penelope, what on earth do you mean?' I gasped. But I did not need to wait for an answer. In a swift, blinding flash of certainty, I knew. She intended to kill me.

'Yes,' she hissed. 'You are going to die. Like *she* did. Nicholas is mine. Nobody is going to have him but me: *she* took him from me and so she had to die—'

'You!' I managed to gasp. 'It was you who killed Mrs Tangye—'

'Of course it was,' she cried. 'She was no good for Nicholas; a trollop that's what she was; and you are no good for him either. I am the woman he must have, I who have loved him all these years...' her voice broke on a half-sob and pity for her mingled with my terror.

'I will go away,' I began, 'and never return—'

'No,' she interrupted. 'He would come after you...he does not see yet that it is I whom he loves; this is the only way.' She came towards me menacingly, her face a mask of insane hatred: 'You shall not escape *this* time, Miss Pearce; I shall not fail like the bungling old fool Polglaze—Oh yes,' she went on, seeing the realization in my eyes. 'I put her up to it; not that she needed much persuasion, she hates you almost as much as I do—'

Of course! How could I have been so blind? Why, oh why had it not dawned on me; had not Jenny told me of the two of them talking together...oh if only I had realized...if only I had confided in Nicholas instead of suspecting him...a wave of shame filled me that I had ever for one single moment doubted him. But it was too late now...I looked round wildly for means of escape. Only then did I realise that the madwoman was nowhere to be seen. Hope surged through me at the thought that perhaps she might bring help. It must have shown on my face.

'Do not build up false hopes of the old hag bringing help,' Lady Penelope sneered, seizing my arm. 'She is as mad as a hatter; no one will listen to her. Do you think I would have let her escape me otherwise?'

There was a reasoned argument about the words that brought the chill of despair.

What happened next was a nightmare. Muttering that she had wasted enough time already, Lady Penelope began to pull me towards the balcony; I could hear the waves thundering on to the rocks far below us...nearer and nearer...the low, iron railings were but a few feet away.

In a last desperate struggle I tried to reason with her. 'If anything happens to me you will be suspected at once,' I cried out. 'The servants knew we both came here.'

She laughed harshly. 'I shall say that you fell or that the mad one pushed you; no one will doubt my word.'

From somewhere I found the power to scream. I screamed at the top of my voice. Again she laughed cruelly. 'No one will hear you you stupid girl.'

The railings were only inches away... I closed my eyes as she forced me against them...a paralysing terror consumed me...I swooned and knew no more.

When I regained consciousness I was lying in Nicholas's arms. For a moment I could not believe my senses. I thought

I must be dreaming for many times in my dreams he had held me so. Then memory came flooding back and trembling violently I clung to him in terror. With infinite gentleness he stroked my hair. 'You are safe now, little one,' he murmured tenderly.

'Lady Penelope,' I cried. 'Where is she? Don't let her come near me—'

'She will never come near to you again, or anyone else,' Nicholas told me quietly. 'She has gone to the death she planned for you.'

I shuddered with horror at his words, the nightmare once more flashed before my eyes. 'But I don't understand...' I began.

'It was the madwoman who saved you,' he explained.

'But you?' I interrupted. 'How did you come to be here; you went to Newquay...'

Nicholas explained what had happened. He had gone to Newquay, as arranged, and in the late afternoon had, quite by chance, come across the Harfords.

'She said they had been called away,' I put in.

'A pack of lies,' Nicholas replied. 'As I soon found out when I mentioned your visit to the castle; neither Sir William nor

255

Lady Marion sent you that letter!'

'Then it was Lady Penelope herself...'

'Without doubt. She must have known the Harfords were away—they were on their way back when I ran into them—and seized the opportunity to get you alone: anyway, when I spoke to them I realised at once that something was wrong...that somebody, I wasn't absolutely sure who, although I had my suspicions, had set a trap for you. I set off for the castle at once and arrived just in time to find the madwoman and one of the servants lifting you from the floor; the sight almost paralysed me with fear—' his voice faltered and I looked at him wonderingly, hope surging within me...

'Oh my darling,' he went on, 'I don't know what I would have done if anything had happened to you...' The sea-blue eyes gazed ardently into mine and I knew that he loved me. Oh the joy, the indescribable bliss that filled me at that moment. The doubts, the fears, the terror of that evening faded as though they had never been. He bent his head and our lips met... Never until I die shall I forget the wonder and ecstasy of that first embrace... At last Nicholas raised his head.

'I have wanted to do that almost since the day I first saw you,' he confessed with a characteristic grin.

'Oh Nicholas,' I cried. 'If only you had done so, what heartache you would have spared me.'

'Had I done so, my little one, you would have shied away like a startled faun,' he teased gently. 'Why, you could hardly bring yourself to accept breakfast from me, remember? I knew I was right to curb my impatience.'

'Perhaps,' I conceded, nestling closer to him. 'But oh you can never know how I have longed for you to say that you loved me.'

'I love you, Carenza,' he said tenderly and kissed me passionately again.

'And I you,' I said softly in return.

But there were more explanations to make. We had to bring ourselves back to earth. I asked where the Harfords were and was told that they were back in the castle; they had come immediately after Nicholas himself and were now with the madwoman; she was in a shocked state and they were trying to calm her. It was from her ramblings that Nicholas had gleaned what had happened. She had heard my

257

screams and had run back to the room to find Lady Penelope trying to push me over the balcony; she had come to my rescue (because, as she said, she liked me) and in the struggle which ensued, Lady Penelope herself had lost her balance and fallen over the low railing.

'Did she tell you anything that Lady Penelope had said?'

Nicholas shook his head. 'No. But she kept rambling on about it being "like the other one" which made me wonder...'

'About your first wife? So you had an idea...'

'It was nothing so certain as that, just a stirring of a suspicion...that was why I kept up some semblance of friendship with her. I thought she knew something...'

'Well you were right. She confessed to me. She murdered your first wife and she was going to murder me. She was in love with you herself as you must surely have been aware.'

Nicholas shrugged. 'I'm not so sure that it was me she was in love with,' he declared, a little cynically. 'More likely my estate and money; she was in rather desperate straits financially.'

Words I had overheard between the two

of them came back to me.

'Did you offer to lend her money,' I asked.

'As a matter of fact, yes,' I was told. 'But how on earth did you know?'

At once I explained, admitting ruefully that I had placed a very different construction on what I had heard. 'I thought you regretted marrying me and had fallen in love with her,' I explained.

'Little goose.' He ruffled my hair. 'Marrying you was the one thing I shall never regret.'

I wanted to know why he had insisted on marriage right at the beginning.

'I wanted to be sure of not losing you. I was afraid that if you stayed at Trenance as nurse, sooner or later you would hear the rumours about me, that I was suspected of murdering my first wife, and would leave. I wasn't prepared to risk that for the simple reason that I had fallen head over heels in love with you at our very first meeting.'

'Oh my darling, dearest Nicholas,' I breathed. 'If only I had known that.'

Suddenly I realised that I had not told him my wonderful news. But it seemed he already knew. 'We found the letter, I and the Harfords. They had suspected all along that you belonged to their brother, but could not bring themselves to accept the fact that he could have behaved in such a manner; they tried to convince themselves that you belonged to Rupert Hanson.'

'I wonder why my father kept his marriage a secret?'

Nicholas told me what the Harfords had said about the matter. They thought Rupert had not dared to tell his father because the old man had been almost fanatical in his desire for both his sons to marry Cornishwomen. Rupert would, of course, have had to break the news at some time or other and was perhaps awaiting the right moment: and then he was drowned...the letter must have been written on the very day...the madwoman must have seen him...or perhaps found it afterwards, for it was never despatched...as there was no mention of the coming of a child it would appear that he had not known about it...

'My poor, poor mother,' I wept. 'I can picture her waiting, alone, hopefully at first, then desperately...'

'Try not to dwell upon her sadness,'

Nicholas said tenderly. 'Remember the joy and happiness the two of them shared in loving each other, even if for so brief a time; in that, you will find comfort.'

I knew he was right and resolved to try to follow his advice; there was neither virtue nor reward in dwelling morosely on the past for either of us...the future, filled with love and promise, lay before us.

EPILOGUE

Lady Penelope's body was never recovered from the sea; the tide must have carried it far out or swept it into some hidden, remote cave or crevice...

I have often wondered about the events of that fateful day and the letter she sent me. She must have known that the Harfords would be away from home and it is more than likely that she knew of my intention of visiting the castle on that day; Mrs Polglaze had heard me telling my plans to Mrs Bray and could have passed on the information.

We have not been able to find out for certain about it because Mrs Polglaze disappeared on the very same night that the tragedy occurred; she must have left Trenance House the minute she heard the news...

However, we have learned from young Bray that Lady Penelope often rode on the cliffs near our home and had been seen talking to Mrs Polglaze on several occasions. His mentioning of this fact reminded me of the day I myself saw her carriage there. It looks as though there must have been some sort of arrangement between the two of them...

I have said nothing to Nicholas about the two attempts on my life. I shall never forgive myself for the momentary suspicion I had of him and the memory of it is the only cloud on my otherwise perfect happiness.

I have asked him about the men in Penzance though, and confessed my fears that he was engaged in smuggling with them. He seemed highly amused at this and not at all angry.

The men, it appears, once came to his aid when he was attacked by a couple of highway-men, and in gratitude to them he told them about the cave with its secret exit (on land owned by Nicholas) which, as he said, might prove handy to them in an emergency... It is clear to me that he is more than a little in sympathy with the 'fair traders' as I might have expected him to be.

The mad woman still roams the moor and we see her from time to time; needless to say, she will always occupy a very special place in our affections.

Whether she was the ghost or not is difficult to say. She may have been, but there are no more 'tappings' on the nursery window—at least Jenny who has come back to us says not—and I have come to think that the ghost was invented by Lady Penelope as part of her plan. Perhaps she cherished the hope that Nicholas would be driven into marriage with her if desperate for someone to look after little Piram.

Nicholas and I are mildly friendly with the Harfords now and exchange visits with them occasionally. From them I have learned the facts about the portrait my grandmother saw in Tregonning Castle: it was a painting, not of my father, but of old Sir Rupert, my grandfather, who had been a friend of the Tregonning family for many years. The resemblance between father and son, I was told, had been quite pronounced. I am to inherit a large sum of money from the Harford estate, my father's share in fact. It appears that old Sir Rupert died soon after his son was drowned and the will was never altered. I understand now the real reason for my uncle and aunt's animosity towards me; it was the threat of the loss of a considerable part of their wealth, rather than the dishonouring of their brother's name which prompted them to disown me!

Try as I will, I cannot feel any real affection for them. Though outwardly pleasant and friendly towards me now, there is neither warmth nor sincerity in their attitude and I fear that they will always, at heart, resent me.

When we first heard about my inheritance, Nicholas remarked wryly that the Harfords and others besides will say that he married me quickly because he had guessed who I really was... Personally I do not think that such talk will arise but Nicholas says that my faith in human nature is unrealistic and naive. He has reason for cynicism I know, but I cherish the hope that our happiness together and my love and devotion for him will eventually serve to free him from such an attitude.

My love for him increases daily and he is far and away above the god-like hero of my past day-dreams.

He loves me with a passionate intensity that is beyond anything I could have imagined, and although I know that life with him will not always be easy or plain sailing, I know that it will be all that I shall ever want in this world.

He teases me abominably, but it is a gentle, playful sort of teasing, laced with love and tenderness, and although sometimes I pretend to be indignant at heart I find it most agreeable...

The portrait he talked of on the day he asked me to marry him has been painted and hangs in our drawing-room.

Nicholas never seems to tire of looking at it and has, as he said he would, called it: Girl From The Sea.

The publishers hope that this book has given you enjoyable reading. Large Print Books are especially designed to be as easy to see and hold as possible. If you wish a complete list of our books, please ask at your local library or write directly to: Dales Large Print, Long Preston, North Yorkshire, BD23 4ND, England.

try to worm you into our good graces. Well, we'll have none of it. None of it, do you hear!'

I backed away from him fearfully, as fists clenched, he leaned menacingly towards me. 'Out of my sight, girl, and never let me hear of you or see you again; and if I hear of your repeating so much as one word of what it says in this infamous letter again, I swear I'll have you transported.' His face mottled with rage he went on. 'A bastard, that's what you are, a bastard trying to profit from a stolen locket.'

He was marching me towards the great door as he spoke. He opened it and pushed me outside. I fell, weeping, to the ground. Slowly, painfully, I stumbled to my feet. Only then did I realise that I had left both the locket and the letter in Sir William Harford's possession. I put up my hand to bang once more on the great oak door then let it fall back at my side. What was the use. Let him keep them. Of what use were they to me now? My grandmother had made a mistake and my dreams of belonging to this great family were without foundation.

I turned despondently away, wrapping my cloak closely about me against the cold.